Our Struggle For Normalcy

By

Yujeong Lee

TABLE OF CONTENTS

1939-6-24

"Come on!" I yell when Rena can't keep up with me. We have to go buy food from the corner shop nearby. Mama told us that we had to get fish and some berries.

Rena is following me as always, getting sidetracked at every turn. Our town is small, so the walk from one end to another is only around half an hour. And the walk to the store isn't long. It is only a ten-minute walk, and I enjoy it. I look at the flowers nearby, small patches of grass growing through the cracks in the sidewalk, and neighbors taking a walk. I hear the normal tweeting of birds, the chirping of cicadas, and the rushing of leaves in the wind. This is normal.

Getting to the store takes twice as much time as usual because of the many times that Rena gets sidetracked, and I have to get her back. She keeps running into the bushes because 1. She saw a bird, 2. Saw a cat, 3. Saw a bug, 4. Saw a butterfly and so on and so forth. There are more things that got her distracted, but they all fit into those four categories.

After I get everything we need, the total cost for Mama's groceries is around 10 zloty, which isn't very high. With a few cents left, I buy mixed candy for me and Rena.

We are heading home now, and I have to almost drag Rena back home because I don't have the energy to stop at every living creature we meet on the path home.

1939-7-1

The teacher is saying something about a unit I don't understand, and I get passed a note: *Wanna meet up at the park later? Sign your name if you're in!*

There is a list of people's names signed under the question: Anders, Grethe, Greta, Hailee, and Frederick. I proceed to put my name there too.

As soon as class ends, I run to the other building to pick up Rena. I have to hurry if I don't want to miss my group at the park, but I promised Mama that I will take care of Rena.

Rena runs out of the building, and I proceed to tell her, "I'm meeting up with friends at the park and if you're quiet and nice, I'll buy you some candy." I show her the few cents I have in my pocket. She looks ecstatic and determined to get that candy. But I know that look, she will try her best, but everything she wants to say will spill out in at least 10 minutes.

My friends are up ahead, and Rena is trying her best to keep quiet. They are waving for me to come quicker. "Come on, we've been waiting *forever*," they say, annoyed.

Hailee adds, "and why'd you bring your sister?"

3

"I always bring her."

"It's not a good idea," Grethe warns.

"Mama asked me. I have to bring her."

Greta sighs, "Fine, but not tomorrow."

As time passes at the park, I notice Rena becoming more and more fidgety. I want her to stay still but she just isn't listening.

"What's wrong?" I ask, but she just shakes her head. I don't think much of it and follow my friends.

Frederick is always the one with the rumors and when he knows something, we know too. As we walk, Frederick says, "So, there is this new teacher coming."

"Really?" I respond.

"Yup."

"So, what are they teaching?" As soon as I say that, Rena taps me on the shoulder and motions that she needs to use the bathroom. I want to stay, but our house is a long walk and if I don't head out now, Rena's going to cause an accident. I start walking away and signal to my friends that I have to go.

Rena looks anxious to go home, so we start running. Our house is still five minutes away, but if we run, we can make it in two. When we finally get home, I get our key from under the mat and we head inside. Rena goes straight to the bathroom, and I head up to my room.

Mama and Father will be here soon and I head to my room to work on my homework. Rena will probably end up playing with some toys or something. Mama comes home in the evening and starts making us dinner. We have all been craving pierogies and today is the day we have them. I help Mama get the food ready and she asks, "how's school?"

4

"Great."

"Anything new?"

"Nope."

"You did take care of Rena after school, right?"

"Yes, sadly."

Then Rena comes running in with Father for the meal.

Rena brags about how she was silent the whole time she was with me and how she can now stay silent for the rest of the day. We're all a bit suspicious, but we agree with her anyways. The food is delicious as always and we talk about the things we did today.

Mama is a teacher at our school and my father works in a nearby hospital. Frederick is in one of her classes. He seems to be one of the annoying ones (I mean he is). He is gossiping all the time and disrupting the class trying to be funny. I think that Greta might be in her class, but I don't know very much. I'm not as close with her as the others, so I don't exactly know if she has Mama as her teacher.

As I finish my plate, I put it in the sink and head to my room. Although I share it with Rena, we have a strict line between my things and hers. I have my basic books and writing utensils while Rena has a bunch of toys. She should really start to get her own utensils or study tools instead of borrowing mine every single day.

1939-7-2

The next day, I wake up and start to get ready for school. I have to wake up earlier than Rena because I have more to get ready for. I get my uniform on and tidy up my hair. When I'm halfway finished, I wake Rena to get her ready. She will wear her uniform, and I will do her hair for her. (She tried once and failed miserably.)

When she wakes up, she is groggy, and she instinctively takes her route to the bathroom to get herself ready. She needs to brush her teeth and put on her uniform. Then I'll tie her hair, and we will head out.

After a long, groggy morning getting ready, we head to school. It takes about 7 minutes to walk to the school. We still have plenty of time before school starts and I want to get there early. Rena is still half asleep and I need to motivate her. (I like doing it though.)

We're almost at the school when I see Rena's teacher greeting people at the door. I send her off and I head to my own school which is 3 minutes away. We go to different schools because of the age difference, and I'm thankful for that. I don't want her following me around, although she might gain popularity in other friend groups.

When I get to class, everyone is talking about the new gossip, chatting about who and who are together now. I get my pencil and my textbook out from my table. Then I join in on the gossip.

"What's happened?" I ask, half expecting to hear that some couple broke up. Someone is always breaking up.

"Oh, someone broke up, but we don't know who," Greta replies.

"What year?" I ask. I knew it.

"Someone in 14," Greta responds, sounding like she couldn't care less.

"Cool." Same for me, I couldn't care less.

"There's so much gossip!" Rya almost shouts. She is the one person who cares too much about other people's lives.

"Yeah," Dau adds. Since he is just Rya's sidekick, he always responds to Rya. Even if it doesn't need a reply.

The teacher walks into the class and we hurry back to our seats. Today's lesson is about the English language, and we learn about the same old boring grammar again. We started learning English last year. As soon as we got into the middle school unit, we were required to take English. Only a few of us are fluent and most of us just know the bare minimum. I'm one of the people who just does the bare minimum.

The class feels like forever and when it's finally over, we have math right after. Math is better than English but it's still quite boring. However, I'm good at it. I take my class with the older kids because apparently, I'm gifted. In class, I try not to stand out as much as possible. The older kids don't understand why a younger kid is there and I don't want to get bullied by the older kids.

The one particular classmate that seems to hate me from the core is Filip. However, there is one person who is kinder to me than the others and she is Aleksky. She's been kind to me ever since I moved up to the higher math class, but the others don't like me very much. They think that I think that I'm better than them and they don't like not being the smartest one in class.

Today's class is just like the others, and nothing's changed in the way the others view me. I want to hide from view, but I can't. And Aleksky is out today, so I have no one to talk to. The teacher adores me (which is not a good thing) and keeps calling on me because I seem special. I know being adored by the teacher is good, but I still don't want to be hated by the others. Class will end in about 5 minutes, so I just have to stay quiet and run back to my regular class as soon as this is over.

6 minutes later our teacher says, "Okay class is over, and be sure to do the homework!"

Everyone agrees and I start to run out as fast as I can.

"Where are you going?" Filip asks. He sounds like he is mocking me.

"Back to my class," I say this in a way that can only be described as rushed and unhappy.

"Oh, the younger weird kid's class," Filip retorts.

"Nope, I'm not dealing with this today," I blurt out and proceed to walk away as fast as I can.

I soon see my class and remember that we have lunch, and I could have just headed outside. "Oh well, now I can take my time."

I put my things down at my desk, and I slowly head outside. Everything is so peaceful. I can hear the birds twittering, the hum of bees, it's amazing. I am listening to the sound of nature, or as I call it, the sound of peace, then I hear a sound of hatred.

"What are you doing here?" Filip says, disgusted.

"I don't even want to be here, and you know it," I shoot back.

"Well, guess we both don't get what we want today." He almost sounds glad.

Of all the days, why today, I think to myself as I walk down the stairs to the outside. Apparently, today is that day once a month when the schedule is wonky, and I have to spend lunch with the guy who hates my guts. Aleksky isn't even here, so I have to be all alone being pestered by Filip. I really hate today. I was already dead inside because of math, and now my spirit is as dead as can be.

I'm outside, sitting by the foot of a tree. I always sit here whenever I'm stuck with the older group. I would have brought a book, but I forgot. Now, I have nothing to do except stare into space and think about what I'll do with Rena later today. I promised her that I would take her out on an outing to the nearby park she loves. I thought that I could buy her a treat on the way there and take a walk and talk on the way back. Although Rena can be very annoying sometimes, she can also be very smart and understanding. She understands more than others think that she will.

While I am thinking, a run-down ball comes hurtling my way.

"Hey! Watch it!" I shout, trying to figure out who did it. And of course, the snickering comes from... *drumroll please...* Filip! I mean who else. And if it was anyone else, it would have been one of his minions. He missed me, but I have this feeling that he's not done. I shift my gaze and say no more. I hear them mocking me, but I shouldn't care. That's what Aleksky said anyway. "Act like you don't care, then at one point, they'll get bored." I have to at least try and live by that.

I go back to my thinking, but now I'm thinking about the most useless things ever, like *What's for dinner? I wonder if the two people who broke up in 14 are back together? What lesson is my class doing right now?,* and more. I think that there are about 3 minutes left of recess, and then I can head back to my class. I just have to survive 3 more minutes, and I can go back to a classroom of normal people who don't hate my guts.

3 more minutes, 3 more minutes, I say to myself, counting every second.

Then I hear the sweet sound of "We're going in, get your things!" I almost trip while trying to get to the door the fastest. As soon as the door opens, I dash to my class with my friends. I am finally free from Filip! I see that my class just ended its period, and we only have one class left before we leave the school.

I call out to Grethe, who just happens to be right by the door. She looks at me and calls, "Hey, come on, school is almost over!"

"Like I don't know!" I call back.

"Come on! We have English next!" She sounds hurried.

"Are we late?" I ask.

"Nope, but there is the most gossip at the start of the class!" Then she runs off.

"Well, guess I'm alone again," I grumble to myself and walk to the English classroom.

Our Struggle for Normalcy

When I'm finally there, the class has already started, and I silently walk to my seat. We are doing introductory words again like Hello and Thank You. We learned this before like 7 million times. We know this by heart now, and I just think the teacher has nothing else to teach us.

Class soon ends and I head to the lower grade section to pick Rena up and take her to the park. By the time I get to the younger grade's section, Rena looks hyped and fully ready to go. As soon as she sees me, she runs over to me full speed. I am not surprised that she is this excited, and we start heading to the nearby park. There are newspaper stands nearby where we can buy some treats for the both of us.

After about 2 minutes of walking, I see a newspaper stand up ahead and see that they do have candy. I run up to them and get a few pieces of mixed candy. The kind that me and Rena both like! I get the strawberry and the cherry flavor, then pay for it.

I wonder if there are any newspapers that I can get for my parents. All I see is the same political stuff. The ones that say stuff about *Hitler in Germany, the greatest Führer of them all* and things like that. Today's article is about how Jewish people are escaping Germany to be safer and how one of the escape boats is now nowhere to be seen.

I don't think much of it, but I buy the newspaper and cram it into my bookbag. I hurriedly run back to Rena, who yells, "Ewa, come on! We don't have all day!"

I run back and give Rena half of the candy I bought. We have the habit of getting an even number of candies and sharing them equally, so we don't fight over any of them. As I give her her half, she looks up at me expecting me to start talking nonstop about my school day. I mean that is what happens every time, so... yeah. Now, I have to tell her everything!

11

<<Note from Rena>>
I actually enjoy listening
about Ewa's school life!

So, this happened, and this happened and Filip is so annoying and this also happened and Aleksky wasn't here and I was so sad and this also happened and that happened… I go on for quite a while. Today wasn't as exciting as other times, (like the time I actually got hit in the face by that wretched ball), but Rena seems engaged in the conversation quite a bit. She is nodding along to my stories and her eyes have a sparkle that I only see when she is with me.

In about 2 hours, my summary of my school day is finished, and I feel so glad that I said everything to Rena. Rena seems like she had a good time listening to me. Although, I half expected her to be sound asleep by the time I finished. When I am done talking, Rena tells me a summary of her day. She met up with her friend Halina when she went to school and ate a simple lunch and came out of school. To her it was the most boring day in the world. I had the most annoying day in the world, and she had the most boring day in the world! So LUCKY!

"We have to get back," I say to Rena. The sun is going down and the night is coming.

"But I don't want to!" Rena whines.

"Soon, Mama will worry about where we are and we'll most likely get yelled at for coming home so late," I tell her. Rena has no other option but to agree. We have a 5-minute walk back home, and a few pieces of candy left to eat on the way.

By the time we get home, dinner is ready and we all sit down and eat together. There's not much special about it except the fact that both of my parents look really tired. Reading the room,

Our Struggle for Normalcy

Rena and I quickly finish our meals and head to our room. Before I leave the kitchen, I give the newspaper I bought to Mama.

In my room, I see a pile of homework from the past week. I kept thinking *it will be fine if I skip one day* and now here I am with a mountain of homework. Overwhelmed by this, I go to the bathroom to take a shower first. I'm probably not even going to start it today, so I'll get ready for bed after I shower. As I start to go to the shower, I start thinking to myself *If I start working now when I'm not really rested, I could probably make the final worse and I go till Thursday and today is Tuesday, so I have all of Wednesday and I'll be rested when I start on Wednesday…*

Later, I go to my bed and look up to the ceiling. Rena is reading a chapter book on her bunk. She seems tired.

"Go to sleep. We have school tomorrow," I say and I doze off as well.

Around 4 a.m., I wake up for some reason. I go to the kitchen to get some water. Whenever I wake up in the middle of the night, I get really thirsty. I walk really lightly so as to not wake my parents and go down to the kitchen. The light is on, which is surprising.

Is it actually 4 am? I think to myself. *If it isn't, why is the light still on? Did someone forget to turn the light off?* I'm thinking about these things when I hear my parents talking.

"Did you read the paper that Ewa bought us?" Mama says.

"Yes, I did," Father replies.

"So, you must know about the boats that take kids from Poland to England." Mama seems scared.

"Yes, and it is a great idea, and we should send them," Father replies in the most nonchalant way possible. *Do you even care about what is going to happen to your daughter?!*

"We should, but Ewa and Rena both have so many friends here!" Mama says in a worried tone.

I guess it is true that I have friends here, but I would love to be 1565.1 kilometers away from Filip. There is also the fact that it is farther away from Germany, where all the war stuff is happening. I have lost all the thought about being thirsty and just stand by my door, listening in for every word that involves me in it. Most of the conversation is back and forth between Mama and Father going on about whether they will send me and my sister on that boat.

I get tired around 4:40 a.m., so I go back into my own bunk.

1939-7-3

The next morning, I do my whole routine of getting up and waking up Rena. Normally, I would chat to myself and talk about the upcoming school day; I would wonder what will happen today, what the new gossip will be and so on. But today, the only thoughts are: *Are they really thinking of sending me away on a boat? They know I have motion sickness; it will be worse on the sea!*

I wake up Rena and she seems as happy as can be. Probably a late effect of all the sugar she ate yesterday. I don't think much of it and start packing my school bag. I pack Rena's as well to speed up the process.

Rena is done getting ready in 10 minutes and I pick up my bag and hers and start heading out the door. Rena is barely following me. I must be walking faster than usual. I try to slow down but end up going even faster. My head is so full of thoughts that my body is going on auto-drive. Rena just whines and keeps asking me to slow down. "We're almost at school! Just keep it up a bit more, okay?" I don't even know what I'm saying.

Once we're at school, I take Rena to her section of the school, and I walk to my section.

When I get there, everyone is looking at me like I just teleported there. I must have walked silently and fast too. I then go to my classroom and get my stuff out. I try to go with the flow, so I don't act all suspicious, but it's hard. There are so many things on my mind right now, that I don't even know what to do with them.

When the teacher comes in, I try to drown out my thoughts with the knowledge being taught right now, but you can't do that if you haven't ever done it before in this class. I try to participate, but I fail miserably every time. I just wait to go outside and talk to my friends. I still have a few classes, but it's okay. *It'll be fast if I daydream for most of the class.*

<<Note from Ewa>>
It did not go fast.
Instead, it took forever.

As soon as the bell for the lunch break rings, I pretty much run out of class. I expect Hailee to be the first one outside. I get my lunch box and sprint down the hallway to go outside. Hailee was still in the classroom when I left, so I should have enough time to get to our usual area first.

I really want to ask my friends about the boats in private. I don't want Rya or Dau to find out. If Dau finds out, Dau will tell Rya and Rya will tell everyone in the school, twisting the words to sound like I'm a monster. But she does it to everyone, not only me. Most people in the school hate her, but she is the daughter of someone important, (I don't know who), and we don't want to cause a fight.

I get to our specific tree. We have our names carved out on one side of the tree marking it as our's. (It's kind of childish, but we like it!) It says: This is the meeting area for Frederick,

Grethe, Greta, Ewa, Anders, Hailee, ~~Rya and Dau~~. The look of it isn't the neatest but considering that it was carved by 10-year-olds with a random rock from the ground, it means something. Rya and Dau's names were scratched out for obvious reasons. Breaking of Rule #1: What happens by the tree stays by the tree. We have lots of gossip that happens here that CANNOT be told to ANYONE. But the very minute things got interesting, Rya and Dau... well, told everyone. And that is why they cannot join us.

```
          <<Note from Rya>>
    All I did was tell a few people,
        but then everyone knew...
            It's not my fault!

          <<Note from Ewa>>
              Yeah, it is!
        You told a few people!
```

I wait for a few minutes, and everyone starts coming my way. I quietly wait for them to come to the tree. When they finally arrive, they are chatting as always.

"So, then they broke up! Right in the middle of the hallway!" Frederick sounds like he is about to jump to the moon.

"Why are you so happy that they broke up?" Hailee replies, sounding more annoyed and tired.

"Just because..." Frederick says it so quietly, we can barely hear him. "Anyways, what do you want to talk about, Ewa?" He says. I can see that he is desperately trying to change the subject about his crush that we already know about.

```
            <<Note from Ewa>>
  He doesn't know that we know, but he
always gets loose when tired, so we got
   him to run around the school for a bet
   and asked him all kinds of questions.
  And we found out. He has no memory of
that, and it is quite funny to watch him
     try to cover up his "secret" crush.
  Don't worry, we're not bullying him, we
     played a game where the group would
  choose a bet for each other to finish.
    No complaints. Mine was to sing a
    childish song at full volume while
   standing on a tree stump. It was so
                embarrassing!
```

Anyways, back to the actual conversation.

"How on earth did you know?" I reply, startled.

"You're always at the tree first if something is on your mind and you've been quiet all day! If that doesn't tell you, what does?" Frederick says this in the most know-it-all way possible. His voice has this haughty tone in it.

"Well, guess that says it," I reply and start talking nonstop about the boats, giving all the information I know about them and what they are and what they're used for and pretty much all my inner thoughts come pouring out of me.

As soon as I'm done pouring my heart out, Greta looks startled and most of the others do as well. We never talk about serious topics, so this is the first time any of us has said anything about the war that is going on right now.

Grethe is the first to speak, "My mom was talking about that too."

"Same here," Anders says quietly. He almost never speaks, so this was a huge moment for us.

"I heard about it and read about it in the newspaper and such, but never actually gave it much thought," Frederick says in the midst of everyone mumbling about hearing their parents talk about the boats. We are all discussing this matter when Rya and Dau come up to the tree.

"What is up with the gloomy faces?" They sound so obnoxious that I want to punch them. But I can't because that would send me to the principal's office. (I never want to do that ever again.) I stay quiet and most of the others give Rya the death stare. Rya seems a little annoyed and scared that we are all looking at her and trying to tell her to go away.

Then the bell rings and we have to start heading in.

"Hey, we're always here for you if you need any help or want to talk about something," Frederick says and starts walking to the door. I silently follow. My head is fuller of thoughts than this morning! I talked to my friends thinking that there would be less to think about and that it would help ease the worry, but NO, it did not help with anything! Now, there is more than ever to think about! I also think that I can't think right! I just want to go home.

The day went by so fast! I forgot what was happening and the classes were probably something important! (Most likely not but what if they were!) I am so worried about this that I might explode! I'm glad that school is over, and I feel a little, just a little, better than this morning.

I go to pick Rena up from the younger grades and start heading home.

"Hey, you're better now!" Rena exclaims while we are walking home. I guess she did notice after all that I had things on my mind.

"I thought you were mad because I ate the leftover candy that you left on the table before you took a shower!" Rena said, sounding as happy as ever.

"Wait, you ate my candy?!" I exclaim. *I didn't even think about the candy because of the boat thing!*

"You didn't know? I'm sorry!" Rena yells and starts sprinting to our house. *It is true that I didn't know, but I'm not really mad about it. I wasn't going to eat it anyway.* I start to run as well because I have to catch up with Rena now.

By the time I catch up with Rena, we are already close to home, so we just run the rest of the way anyway. When I go in, I don't see anyone, so I head to my room to work on some homework.

Around the time I'm done with homework, I hear Mama cooking in the kitchen and Father walking around the house. Rena has already run out to greet them, and I stay in my room because I still have homework to finish.

Dinner is quick and quiet. No one says much. Rena is the only one who keeps on talking. I want to talk to my parents, but I don't want to talk to them about the boat when Rena is right there.

Rena leaves as soon as she is done eating because she feels awkward talking all alone and thought that she should give the quiet people some space.

<<Note from Rena>>
I hate silence.
It just creeps me out!

20

As soon as she goes to her room and closes the door, I blurt out, "What are you gonna do with us? What about the boats? Why us in the boats? What is going on politically?..." I think I say it too fast because even after I say everything, my parents' faces are all jumbled up trying to comprehend what I said. Then, they say in great length, "So, Hitler is trying to take over the world and one of the theories is that he is going to invade Poland. I know this is all scary and stuff, but I can't feel any reality from it. It's like that feeling when you move but feel like your home is still somewhere else. And now that we know about this, we don't want you to be in trouble, so we want you to be as far from Germany as possible. And there is this boat that will take you to England…." (This explanation took around 10 minutes) In the end, the conclusion is that they have made the decision to send us on the boat the next time it comes to Poland, and it will take me and Rena to England. I kind of agree with that idea, but I don't know if it is the right thing to do. I don't understand everything, but as if my parents notice, they tell me to go back to my room and sleep now. It is true I'm getting tired, so I start to head to my room and try to wrap my mind around what I've heard.

1939-7-4

I wake up, and I wake Rena for school. We do our normal before school routine, packing our bags, and wearing our uniforms. We got ready in 10 minutes and started heading out the door when my father yelled, "Don't go to school today!"

Huh? Father is the type that will make you go to school with a fever and a cough! Education is the most important thing to him! Wait, what? I don't understand a thing that's going on right now, but I have to stay home today? "Rena, we're staying home today." I tell her and we start heading back toward the door.

"So, we are choosing to send you on the boat going to England, and your mother and I will teach you all that we can to help you stay safe, and you will no longer attend this school," Father says. I begin to understand the importance and the reason why we didn't go to school today. "You will learn to tend wounds, make food with limited resources and other survival skills that may help you."

Father starts to get some notebooks for us to take notes. We take the notebooks and wait for more information. "You will be on the boat to England in a month, so we will teach you as much as we can." Father kept going. "And try not to tell your friends about the reason you are not coming to school. The authorities cannot know." Now, I understand how grave this situation is and how important it is to learn as much as we can.

"If this is so important, why are only me and Rena going? Why can't you go too?" I ask. I've wanted to ask this since yesterday. I want my parents to come with me. I want to know why they never include themselves in the boats.

"Because there is paperwork about us in the government. We are adults, so they have our age, gender, how we look, and others. But you are young, and they don't know about you. You will be safer to move around," he says this in a straight face, and this is the part that makes me nervous. He didn't have a sad look or anything, just that face that he has every day. I feel like he is deep in thought but, not having any facial expressions whatsoever is kind of annoying at times.

"So, what are we going to do? Just stay where we are until the boat comes?" I ask. I have to stop asking questions. *I will find out the answers eventually, so I need to restrain my questions! What Father thinks is probably thought out as soon as something dangerous comes up, so it will be fine! I bet that's the reason he is so calm right now!*

"Fine, but what are we going to do first? You told us that we will be doing a lot of stuff that will help us survive right?" I need to ask more questions! Just a little more!

"Yeah, what about English if we're going to England?" Rena pipes up.

How does Rena even know what English is! When I was her age, I thought Polish was the international language for all the world! Does this just mean that she is smarter than me? We didn't start learning English until we got to middle school! No way, she probably searched through my school bag in search of candy and found my English homework! Either way, she knows about English which is good. If she is willing to, I could

23

probably teach her basic words and the alphabet. And I even could get some materials from school to help her… *Wait, I'm not going back to school, so I might have to make the materials myself!* I keep on thinking about how to help Rena with English that I forget my father is trying to teach us.

"It will be great if you help Rena with English! Great idea!" Father said, grinning a bit. I didn't even notice that I was talking to myself! I know I do this sometimes, but I didn't notice it now! *What did I say? Anything inappropriate? Anything offensive? What did I say? What did I say?*

```
<<Note from Rena>>
Ewa was saying all of
    this out loud…
```

It took Father about 20 minutes to calm me down and stop me from talking to myself. I am also drowning out everyone else's voices, so it took some vigorous shaking by the shoulders to get me to listen. I guess I really have to get aware of my surroundings… Anyways… I listen more after that. Father is saying important stuff the whole time, and it will be a pain to go over this again in the future.

Here is a simple summary of how it went:

wwww wwww www ww w www ww w w www www www wwww www wwwwwww wwww ww www wwwww wwwwww ww www www www ww www www w www www www wwww ww wwwwww www w ww w www w ww wwwwww wwwwww wwww www wwww w www ww www www www wwwwwww ww ww www www www ww www www www www

Our Struggle for Normalcy

Welp, I guess I already forgot everything except for a paragraph of jumbled words. Father would be so mad if he found out.

"Today, you most likely want the day to comprehend everything that I've told you today. I will give you the rest of the day. If you meet up with friends, don't tell them about this conversation," Father says this with caution, and I feel a slight pity coming from him. I guess he does feel bad for the situation we're in considering I have friends and all. I should probably not tell him that I told them about the boats already. Wait, should I? I don't know, but I won't think about that today.

I see Rena run outside as soon as Father says we're done. She's probably going to the park nearby, so I grab our run-down kickball, and start heading for the park. I want to have a conversation with Rena but at the same time I need to get some energy out. (Or else I burn myself out with my overthinking.)

When I get to the park, I see Rena climbing a tree. She always climbs the same tree over and over and has a special branch for every mood. One for troublesome thinking, one for sad thoughts, and all the other branches are for happy times. When she is extremely happy, she will be jumping around in the tree, but not going on the sad branch and the troublesome thinking branch. But now, she is on both the troublesome thinking branch and the sad thoughts branch. (Her legs are resting on the sad thoughts branch and the rest of her is sitting on the troublesome thinking branch.) I have never seen her in this position, and this worries me, so I put the kickball down by the foot of the tree and go to the spot that is "easy" to climb. I have never been good at climbing trees, so I am not surprised when I keep on falling on my butt and slipping on everything. Rena looks back at me as I fall for the third time. I get my foot up on a random branch, but I fall backwards as soon as I reach for another branch. Rena starts to come near me. *I suppose she*

25

doesn't want me to intrude on her thinking. But as soon as she comes towards me and sees me struggling to climb the tree, she bursts out laughing. She has to hold onto a nearby branch to not fall from the tree. *Is she making fun of me? She knows I'm not good at climbing trees!* But weirdly, I feel giggly too now! I also burst out laughing and the two of us laugh together.

When we are finally done giggling and laughing our hearts out, Rena comes down the tree and teaches me how to climb the tree, so I can also sit with her. It took some time to get me to understand how to do it, but I can go up the tree now. Rena shows me to the branch she is sitting on. I sit on it too and she sits right next to me.

"Is it true? Am I really going to England?" She asks in a worried tone. "I have friends here! I like people here!"

"I know, I feel the same way, but we will be able to see them again and if lucky, they might come on the same boat!" I say, trying to seem excited. She must have already forgotten about the day I was moody and quiet and walked fast. "It will be fun! We'll drink tea, go to palaces and more!"

Rena's face lit up. "Oh, really! That sounds fun, and talking about fun, you brought the kickball, right?"

"Of course I did, what kind of sister would I be if I didn't? It's at the foot of the tree," I exclaim, a little too loud.

Rena jumps down the branch and grabs the ball and starts to run towards a field. I also try to jump down the tree like Rena but fall flat on my face. *I can't climb trees or come down trees after all.* I wipe the dirt off my face and clothes and start running to catch up with Rena.

Rena is already dribbling the ball and waiting for me to catch up. Unlike Rena, I don't have as much stamina or running speed. I am breathing heavily by the time I get to her. Rena throws me the ball and I catch it. I then throw it back to her and we play with the ball for a while.

Soon, the sun begins to set. "We should be heading back now," I say, then pick up the kickball that I dropped moments ago. Then I start heading the way back to our house. Rena follows behind me.

When we get inside the house, I head straight to my room, Rena still following me. I don't really feel like having dinner today after all that information I was given. I would need to eat, but I don't want to be at the dinner table. I have some candy and snacks stashed up in one of my cabinet closets, so I won't starve. *Probably.*

Anyways, I head to my room to my snack cabinet, searching for something to munch on. "There's probably a pack of gum somewhere here…" I mutter as I rummage through the pile of snacks and the pieces of clothes (I don't wear them of course. I just put it on top so people don't figure it out, especially my sister.)

"Whatcha looking for?" Rena pops up behind me.

"Ahh! When did you get here!" I half scream as I rush to cover the cabinet. I don't want Rena to find out. If she does, she's going to eat it all!

"Hmmmmmm. You sure?" She asks, coming closer to me.

"Yeah, yeah," I stammer. Rena looks at me suspiciously, but then walks away. I'll probably have to change where I put my snacks, but at least Rena didn't find out today.

I keep rummaging through the cabinet and land my hand on a pack of gum, which I take out and start munching on. Then I pick out a book from my shelf and start reading. A random story book that I loved to read when I was younger. I still read it sometimes now, but it's mostly for nostalgia. It's surprising that

I picked this book out of all the books I have today. I guess my subconscious is telling me to relive the past to get through with the present. I guess.

I read the book. The entire story is about when life is hardest, you have to be stronger. (guess I need that). And at the end of the book, a notecard comes out. It is written in the most illegible handwriting, but after some time of struggling, I can kind of read what it says. **Whatever life throws at you, as long as you try hard, you'll be fine.** From my memory, Grandpa wrote this for me while reading this book to me.

Well, after that, I kind of lived on that for my life. I try not to look like a try-hard, but still, I guess I have it in me.

I wake up in the middle of the night again. The lights are off outside, which probably is a good thing. It says 4 a.m. on the clock. I guess I slept through dinner. I see some leftover stew in the pot, so I pour myself a bowl and slurp it down. Guess I am hungry after all. I was a bit hungry when I came in earlier, but I know how to control my hunger. I can keep it up for 5 hours without budging. Well, the stress is coming at me. I mean I am showing all the symptoms of my normal stress routine. I had some sugar, (the gum probably had sugar) slept for some time, and woke up in the middle of the night. So, I'm stressed. I mean can you blame me?

I get some water and drink that as well. I wonder about the living room. There is no one awake, and I can hear crickets in the distance. My anxiety is slowly calming down. I don't even notice the fact that my heart is beating faster than usual, and my temperature is also hotter than usual. Oh, well, I should get some rest, but the sound outside is so calming. I'll probably stay here for a little while longer.

1939-7-5

I probably fell asleep on the couch, and when I wake up, the sun is already up, and I could hear my family walking around the house. I must have slept for at least 5 hours. I should get ready for school now. *Wait,* I'm not going to school anymore. So, I can stay in my PJs.

Father comes out of his room and looks at me like *why are you not ready to go outside right now, get ready.* I got the idea, so I got dressed in my room. I choose the most comfortable thing I can find and come outside. Father motions me to get a basket and wait for Rena. Rena comes out of the house groggily and gives Father the death stare. I guess she wants to sleep longer. It is earlier than any time I wake up for school.

"Today, I am going to teach you about herbal medicine and poisonous herbs. Remember to not eat the poisonous ones," Father says as he starts walking. We seem to be going to the nearby mountain to get some herbs. I guess that's the reason we need baskets. We start walking and I see a dandelion, so I pick it up and put it in Rena's hair. It is a simple ornament, and I even knew what properties a dandelion had. It is edible, no poison, but there is no use to it in medicine. It also tastes pretty bad.

Although it is a flower, it tastes just like grass. I actually quite liked eating it until I ate a bug as well as the flower, so now I don't eat dandelions anymore.

I think about eating once again, but I don't want to eat a bug again. My father stops in front of me. In front of us is a small hill with all kinds of medical herbs that I don't even know the names of. But for one, I know there is nothing venomous or harmful to the human body.

"Gather the herbs that you know the name of," Father says as he starts to gather herbs as well. I start to gather the ones I know of; there are some dandelions, peonies and other flowers I think are edible. But it might not be enough, so I grab a few herbs that I know would help treat a cold. After I am done gathering, I wait for Rena to finish gathering. Father is already done gathering.

We go home and Father gets everything out. I learn more about how to use the materials we got in the most practical way. I love learning about medicine, and I feel so happy that I can learn more. My father was reluctant to teach me medicine in case I made poison... But now! I've learned so much in one day that I think I might be imagining it. I have to stuff it all down. I might hate all learning, but medicine is one of my biggest passions!

What I end up learning is that all the plants I picked are just edible but pretty and the ones my father picked were medicinal herbs that could actually be used to heal someone. We learn more about herbs and by the time Rena gets tired of listening to all the "medical jibber jabber" Father leaves me and Rena to go have the rest of the day to ourselves.

After that, since we have a free day once again, the only thing he asks of us is to study English just a little bit. I get one of the books I borrowed permanently (stole) from the school library, and skim through it. I understand most of it, although I don't understand words like *creative, magical* or *air*. But I have a dictionary with me, so I know what it means now. Now that I've read a few pages of a book, which counts as studying English, I can go out and meet some friends! Father never said anything about meeting them today. He said to not meet up with them yesterday, but not today!

I go by the school because it is going to be minutes before the class ends. By the time I get to the school, people are flooding out of the class. I kind of mix into the crowd acting like I was always here. Then as nonchalantly as possible, I walk behind the crew. They don't notice, so I just follow along. They get to the normal tree and start talking.

"I wonder where Ewa is," Frederick starts.

"Yeah, she's been gone for some time," Greta replies.

"I wonder..." Anders says as he looks around. But then he spots me.

"WAIT! How long have you been here?!" Anders yells as the others spin around.

"How long have you been there!?" Grethe yells.

"Where were you?" Frederick hollers.

"Are you sick with an inevitable sickness or a fate?" Hailee asks a little louder than everyone else. "Wait, are you a ghost of Ewa haunting us?" Greta says being drowned out by the rest of them. And the fact is that they all said this at the same time, and I didn't even know much of it.

So, because they ask, I go on a full rampage about the boats and more. I know I'm not supposed to tell them, but they are my closest friends so, I guess I should tell them.

I told them everything and they seemed like they didn't care. They were just glad that they could see me again. After they were done listening, they just got back to talking about their own stuff. I guess that is what it always is.

"So, anyways the school is boring as always, and you know that guy, what's his name... Pholop? Or is Filop, anyway, he asked me where you were. I mean I didn't know either but what's his deal?" Greta says as she digs through her bag for something. She comes up with a notebook and hands it to me.

"We made a study packet for you since you were gone for so long. Aleksky made the math one. I think this would help you stay on track." Greta says confidently as she bonks me on the head with it.

"Still, you should come to school" Greta says, and others nod in agreement.

"Yeah, but the Marco Polo bridge incident and everything just shows that it's dangerous. I say kind of quietly. To be honest, I want to go to school, everything is good there except that stupid Filip.

"Anyways, what's happening in school?" I ask, and they start a nonstop rant about their school lives and the gossip I missed out on.

So, basically,

And this is all the gossip I missed out on. Yay? I don't even like gossip that much... Well, I am in a group where gossip is life...

The sun is setting, so I say my goodbyes and start to go home and wash up. Father is already in bed, and because I was out for so long, I forgot dinner. But it's fine. I then go to bed and wish for a day just like this for tomorrow.

1939-7-6

As I wake up, I hear Father rustling, and I suspect that he is outside preparing for today's lesson. Considering that the rustling I hear are bandages, he probably is trying to teach us how to stitch up skin or how to bandage a wound.

I dressed quickly and went outside to help Father. He was actually getting scissors and needles. I think that was for the stitching. There was a pillow on one side of the shed and Father was starting to make slits in it. Rena came through the door with a groggy face but as soon as she saw the pillow being torn up, she woke up. She ran to the pillow, grabbed it and took it away. I ran at her and got it back and Father began to explain the reason to it.

I honestly think that this will be great, but I honestly wonder if I could skip today because I want to play with my friends again. I mean, they're not out of school yet, but they have the choice to ditch… Well, and I already know how to stitch. Skin and clothes. I could probably get better, but I can do it. Yup, totally…

Without even asking my father, I pick up the needle and get to it. I make 5 stitches, and I notice that there are splotches of red on the pillow now. Well, guess I poked myself... But there is more red now, and when I finally look at my finger, there are at least 6 or 7 cut marks that are easily seen. And, as you can expect, there is blood starting to ooze out. I mean, I was rushing because I wanted to get more sleep, or at least have some free time. I also want to go check out that math booklet.

I kind of panic when I see blood, so I do the most reasonable thing possible which is yell as loud as you can for your doctor father. And as you can imagine, he comes running. He gets some anesthetic and a bandage to wrap my finger and he is done curing it in less than 1 minute.

He gives me a lecture about how I should be more careful and how to use the needle more neatly. And I do not want to listen through that again. I grumble through the whole thing, although I frickin hate it. But my hand doesn't hurt anymore, which is good. All is good that doesn't kill you, right?

As soon as Father says, "I know that you want to go, so go play!" I run out of the house without looking back. I go look for my friends with a pencil and the workbook they made for me.

I wait for hours on end, but they don't show. They probably had to go somewhere. This kind of thing happens once in a while, but now, I've lost my free day... So, I go home and sulk in my bed.

1939-8-5: A MONTH LATER!

I've learned so much, but I think there is more to learn! I still can't believe that I'm already leaving. I love that I get to be safe and all, but, still. Apparently, Father and Mama have a family friend in England that can help us. We are going to stay with them until the war ends. We need to head on the boat tomorrow.

I pack a bag with my most needed stuff. That includes a pair of clothes, some money and medical tools. I get a bag for Rena too and put one of her most treasured things in there as well. The small keychain that we got when the whole family was out together at a fair. I put some clothes into that one as well and closed the bag.

"This is actually happening" I say to myself as I put it all together in my head. I then lay down on my bed thinking to myself that it's all going to be fine and over before I know it.

1939-8-6

I still can't believe it, but I am heading to the dock with two bags. Rena also has two bags and is walking with a lollipop in her mouth. Yes, I know she is happy as she can be but still feels a bit weird. Mama looks sad and Father looks worried to death. We on the other hand are looking like there is no care in the world.

By the time we are at the dock, we are not the only ones there. Everyone is talking to their kids, reassuring them, and telling them that they will be together soon. I look at Mama, half expecting her to start crying. She does not, but I can clearly see that she is biting her lip very strongly. I mean, I see blood. Father is also looking really far away and not looking at us. But I can see his eyes getting watery. He probably doesn't want to cry in front of us.

"Those going to England, please board the boat now!" says the random person putting down a pathway for us to walk on. I look at Father like *Am I really going?* And as soon as I give him that look, he hugs me really tight. Rena is also stuck in this hug, and I don't care that much. I mean this might as well be the last time I see my parents. But we'll be fine, Mama and Father will come to England as soon as the war is over. And most wars don't last that long. *Right?* It's going to be fine. Mama hands me a hand knitted scarf and Rena a hand knitted beanie. She also hugs us really tight and only lets go at the very last second. As soon as she let us go, we have to run to the boarding place because, well, the random person was starting to fold up the pathway thing.

We manage to get on the boat, and wave to Mama and Father as the boat starts to move. We are slowly moving away from the dock, and I start to see open water. Mama and Father are crying, and I am looking back at them, and I feel my eyes tearing up as well. Rena is by my side and is clutching on to her beanie and crying a bit as well. *I have actually never seen her cry like this. She is always the upbeat person that forgot about things pretty soon.* I hug Rena and put up my smile. I practiced this smile for days before the boat. I didn't want Rena to feel all the pressure, so I practiced making fake smiles that looked real and how to stop myself from crying or having panic attacks. *I literally gave myself panic attacks just so I could practice.*

"Hey, let's go check our rooms," I say in the most upbeat way possible, making it sound like it will be a fun little adventure. I go and take Rena's hand and start to walk to the hallway to our rooms. I look around while I'm trying to find my room. There are people everywhere with bags in their hands looking for their rooms. The boat itself isn't the greatest and a little dirty as well, but it is pretty large.

When we find our room, it is room 349 on the second level. I walk to the hallway and see some people by the door. When I enter the room, I see 4 beds (all bunk beds) and a person by the door.

As I enter the room, I see a free bunk. The one that the person in front didn't claim yet. Rena wants the bottom bunk, so I put my stuff on the top bunk. I don't really care about what bunk I got, so I don't care that much. Rena looks like this is a whole new world and is considering the new circumstances in her head. She could think after all. We sit on our bunks, dazed. We hear the engine of the boat roaring underneath us, and the truth of the situation is still feeling a hundred years away.

I'm still staring into space when I hear someone getting close to our new "room." I look at the door and see Aleksky. Of all people, Aleksky, by the door with a bag in her hand. She seems to be on the boat for the same reason we are. To go to a safer place. I guess we are all on the same boat! Literally. I can;t believe Aleksky is here! She is really here! I'm not alone! I wanted one of my friends to go with me, but I didn't expect us to be in the same bunk together as well! This is so exciting. (But on the other hand, it seems a bit sad).

"Are you really here or am I hallucinating?" I ask.

"Wait? You're here?" Alesksky gasps.

"YAY!" We both exclaim. We are most likely thinking the same thing. We are lucky to be in the same bunk.

```
        <<Note from Ewa>>
     Now that I think about it,
     that's probably the reason
     she didn't come to school
            all the time.
```

I keep thinking about how we are so lucky. But, at the same time, there is Rena that I have to take care of. But I assume that she will like Aleksky. I look up at Rena, and she is looking at me with huge eyes. She probably doesn't even know what we are talking about. She seems to grasp that we are friends but doesn't know which one of my friends she is. However, after the celebration that we are together, we don't talk that much. We can pretty much guess each other's lives beforehand and that we are here because of the same reason.

When I open my mouth again, all I can say is, "Wow, this is really nice," and it is in the most awkward tone ever. I look out the small "window" in our room and see the sun setting. The clock shows that it is around 7:30 pm, so I get Rena and head up to the top to see if there is food.

When we get up there, all I see are a few apples and some oatmeal. I assume that it is free to take, so I get a bowl of oatmeal and two apples. One for Alekscky and one for me. Rena gets the same stuff as I did and starts to eat it as we go back down to the bunk. When I get to the bunk again, I throw Aleksky an apple and head into my bunk. Aleksky seems surprised by the apple and bites into it. It makes a crunch sound, and I bite into mine as well. We are hungry after all. We ate, and didn't think much of the rest.

By the time we finished, it was already 9 pm and I thought that we might as well go to sleep early. *I mean, we have a whole trip ahead of us right?* I'm starting to doze off, but a pile of thoughts is dumped into my head. All the what-ifs are pouring into me. I didn't really expect much, but still. A lot of things happened, and I just kept it in.

I'm thinking and thinking, and I really hope I wasn't saying all this out loud. I'm still thinking but another train hits my brain. And this one is saying, *You're sleepy, You should sleep, Don't you feel tired?* And more. All I can do now is just think about how sleepy and tired I am. Soon, I doze off.

1939-8-7

When I wake up, I instinctively walk to the right of me. Then, I walk into the wall. And in the most comedic way possible. *(Imagine a character walking into a wall and going splat)*. I mean it must have been loud as well because that immediately woke the other two people in the room. Alecksky rubs her eyes sleepily and says "What's going on? Is someone hurt?"

"No, no, I'm fine, I just ran into the wall," I reply. My head hurts really bad but I don't want to worry anyone. It's probably a mild concussion at best. I'll be fine as I eat food and rest. And there is nothing to do here anyway. I go back into bed thinking I'll rest a little bit more.

In about an hour, Rena is shaking me awake. I guess she woke up and she was bored to death. She doesn't know Alecksky and that probably means that she doesn't trust her. If it was anyone else like Fredrick or Grethe, she would have been with them just fine. Anyway, I open my eyes to see Rena looking down at me. I stand up again and walk to the right of me again. I bump into the wall again.

"Ow, that hurts! Not again!" I need to remember that there is a wall on the right of me and that I should stop walking into it or else I'm actually going to get brain damage.

"What do you need?" I say to Rena. I'm kind of annoyed with myself because I crashed into that wall twice.

"I wanna go see the ocean and I'm hungry!" Rena seems annoyed with me. I don't care that much about the ocean, but it is what Rena wants, so I wake myself up and put on some fresh clothes.

After I get changed, I walk to the door, with Rena following me. We walk down the hallway for like forever, and it's really dim, so I don't want to lose track of Rena. I hold on tightly to her hand until I trip on the stairs. And again, I fall in the most comedic way possible. *(I always act so put together, but that's only because I know where things are back home.)* Thank goodness that the stairs didn't go down, or else I would be tumbling down the stairs.

After a lot of tripping, falling and Rena rolling her eyes for the seventh time, we finally are up on the deck. There are still apples left from yesterday's dinner and I toss one of the apples to Rena. Rena catches it and bites into it. With a mouth full of food, she says, "This is fun! Even one of your school friends is here!"

"Who? You mean Aleksky?" I ask in reply.

"No! That guy you always talk about, you know Filip. He's over there!" Rena says. Wait, what, there is absolutely no way he is on this boat! He can't be on this boat! Rena points to the other side of the boat, where I see a familiar figure. I expect that Rena just pointed out someone that looks like Filip. When I see the person Rena is talking about, I see a teenage boy with blondish hair eating an apple. There's no way that it's actually him! I think as I instinctively walk away from that direction. But I am still keeping an eye on that person. I keep track of every move, but the more I look at him, the more I see the resemblance. Then, he looks around, as if noticing the gaze. I am still looking at him, and like I feared, it's him.

"Rena, do you want to go back?" I panic.

"Nah, the drama here is good. I wanna see how this ends," Rena says in a devilish way.

"Please, I'm begging you! Let's go!" Then I pull Rena's arm and start walking back to the stairway. I need to calm myself.

As I am walking to the stairway, I use some breathing techniques that I learned from Father to calm myself down. I am walking down, and Rena follows behind me. I walk to our room/dorm/bunk and sit on the bed. Aleksky is here as well. When she sees me rush into the room, she asks, "Hey, you okay?"

"No! Did you know that Filip was here?"

"Yes, he told me a while ago."

"Then why didn't you tell me?"

"'Cause you were never in school!"

Oh, wait, that makes sense. I haven't been to school for a while. I guess, I can't blame her, and there's nothing I can do now. Because I am stuck on this boat. *Maybe I can jump off and survive?* Nah, it won't work, if anything, I'm going to die in that ocean.

I slump on the bed, still munching on the apple. I keep on thinking to myself about ways to deal with this and come up with one idea that might just help me. Which is: *If I see him, ignore him to my best capability, and if he sees me, try to avoid direct conversation.*

I slap my face a few times and stand up. Rena looks annoyed with me, and I would be annoyed with myself as well. I mean, it would have been amazing drama if I did end up talking to Filip.

"Hey, Rena, Let's go back up. I want to see the ocean."

"Yay! Back to the top we go!" Rena yells as she starts darting outside, running straight to the stairs. I follow her, careful not to trip or fall again.

When I finally catch up with Rena, she is already halfway up the stairs, and I am panting heavily. I really need to work on my stamina.

Rena is running around the deck looking at everything from other people walking around, and other teenage kids. One of the kids finds a box that she can stand on and puts it by the railing on the boat.

She looks out with gigantic eyes, trying to memorize everything. She is gaping at the vast ocean, which to me is pretty boring. I know that it should be cool and everything, but I have seen it a few times before.

I'm looking into the ocean when I feel a tap on my shoulder. I quickly turn around to see Filip. I wish it was anyone else. I would have preferred Rya than him! I see him sneering and I jump back. I know that I would try to avoid him, but I forgot all about it! Maybe this is a good time to jump off the boat. NO, no, I can't, I just have to suck it up.

"Hi," Filip says shyly.

"Hi, what. What do you want from me?" I am annoyed to the maximum.

"Just saying hi…" he says as he starts looking away.

"Okay…" and I start walking away. I don't want to talk to anyone longer than I have to. I grab Rena's arm and start pulling her away. Then I look back at him and shoot him a look that says *I don't like you, so don't act all friendly!*

I don't want to think about this too much. I'll probably not care as soon as I'm off the boat though.

As I walk away from Filip, I try to think of happy things. I may look annoyed, but there is more madness than annoyance. Rena looks at me all weird because I was so mean to him. For all she knows, she thinks I like him! She couldn't be any more wrong. But at least the first hardship on this boat is over. Now, I have to get through the rest of the time on this boat.

I feel a tug on my arm as Rena pulls me away from a nearby staircase. I must have been walking without thinking again and probably at the verge of tumbling down the stairs.

"Thanks, I don't wanna fall again," I thank Rena.

"You're fine but be more careful."

"Sorry, I'm a little scattered right now."

"It's all because of your boyfriend, Filip!" Rena half yells. I couldn't care less about what Rena thinks, but if she yells it to the entire boat, that's going to be a problem. I wish she was a little quieter and would not yell false statements to the entire world.

I get myself together and start walking back to the bunk room. I had my share of Filip for the day.

I walk down the stairs and keep heading down until I see my bunk. Aleksky is sitting on her bed reading a random book. It seems to be from the school library, which she probably stole.

"Aleksky, I'm going to stay here for the rest of the day."

"Sure, why not, it's not my bunk."

"You got another book? I wanna read something."

"Yeah, I got like 5 from the library back at school."

"Ooh, give me something fun."

45

"This one is pretty fun," she says as she throws me a book. I look at the back of it and see a description that says: A comedic story of a girl with a weird hair color. So, basically, it's a comedy book. Ehh, why not. It sounds fun, and I need to kill time. Rena is already taking a nap, and I don't mind.

I read and read and read until my stomach growls. Guess it's already time for dinner. There is nothing to do on this boat except read or stare into space, so I guess the time goes pretty slow unless you're actually doing something.

I wake Rena and grab Aleksky from her book and start walking to the dinner area.

"What? Already? Guess I forgot all about the time," Aleksky says as she starts to walk.

"I'm hungry. I want candy," Rena grumbles.

"There isn't any candy, but there's oatmeal and apples upstairs so suck it up," I say, and I add, "At least we have food, other boats don't."

"Well, still. Oatmeal gets boring," Rena whines.

"Then, don't eat it. You're the one who'll starve. Not me," I say. We are right by the table with the food now, so I hand Aleksky a bowl of oatmeal and get some apples as well. Rena is grumbling but gets a bowl herself anyway. While I am grabbing a bowl, I hear Aleksky talking with someone, so I turn around to see who it is. Of all the people, I didn't expect Filip to be there. One weird thing—he was smiling? I don't think he was sneering/jeering/taunting/mocking/insulting/ridiculing. *(These are all the stuff he does on a normal day to day basis.)* I was surprised. But, still, why was he here? I might as well leave. I take Aleksky's hand and start to pull her back to our room.

"Hey! Ewa!" Filip yells.

"What." I am so annoyed right now!

"I just wanted to say I was sorry for how I acted in school." He seems genuine.

"Apology not accepted." He did make my life hell after all. Then I grab Rena, and Rena grabs onto Aleksky and I pull them back to the way of our room.

As I am pulling them back to our room, I bump into this girl who looks about the same age as I am.

"Sorry!" I say and I start walking even faster, as if to avoid her. Truth be told, I'm avoiding Filip, not her. She looks nice. I keep on dragging Rena and Aleksky along until we are in our room.

"Phew! Away from Filip! But... I feel sorry for the girl I bumped into."

"Gee! If you're so sorry for bumping into a girl, say sorry to us! You literally dragged us down here! And loosen your grip a little!" Aleksky yells at me.

"I'm sorry! I panicked!"

"Fine! But next time, don't drag us along. Rena looks like she has a bruise on her arm!"

"Oh! Rena are you okay?" I ask.

"Yeah, I'm fine," Rena says with a little scowl. They both seem a little annoyed with me for dragging them. I plop down on my bed and dig through my luggage for some candy. Maybe this might help ease the tension.

```
          <<NOTE FROM EWA>>
     I brought a bucket of
       candy from Poland.
```

47

Anyway, after digging for some time, I grab on a lollipop and pull it out. I pull another out and hand one to Rena, and the other to Aleksky. Rena, seeing candy for the first time in two days, takes the candy like a ravenous dog. Aleksky on the other hand seems surprised by the candy but abstains from it. I take a lollipop for myself and lie down on my bed. It is pretty late, and the other woman (whose name I forgot) is already asleep. Oh! That reminds me. I never thought about her long enough, but she seems nice. She gets mad pretty easily, but she is a nice sport. She is fluent in Polish, English and German, and apparently, she's 32 years old. She does not like candy…bummer. And she has a sister, I think. All this thinking is tiring! I might as well just go to sleep.

1939-8-8

Rena is shaking me awake again.

"What do you want? I'm really tired!" I scowl.

"Come on!!!!! Breakfast!!!!!"

"I know! But I want to sleep!"

"Oh well. Come on." As if the roles are turned around, Rena pulls my left arm and drags me out of bed. Then, she starts to drag me out to get breakfast.

As we are walking, I start to wake up little by little. I was expecting to not wake up for some time, so it took some time before I fully woke up. It's not until we are by the stairs when I fully wake up. Rena starts to pull me up the stairs and I walk on my own.

"Finally! I don't have to drag you anymore!" Rena says as she stops pulling on my arm. She lets me walk on my own and starts to walk faster. I start to run to catch up with Rena.

We walk up the stairs and get to the snack table and get some food. We each get a handful and start walking back to our room. We obviously got some for Aleksky as well. As we are heading back down, I see tied brown hair on some girl walking by me. *Reminds me of the girl I bumped into yesterday.* That reminds me that I should probably apologize to that girl I bumped into yesterday. I feel really bad... I have nothing else to do today, so I probably will go search for that girl and apologize.

We are back in our room before I even notice, so I bite on an apple and rummage through my bag for a lollipop. I want to give it to her as a sign that I'm sorry. Rena is like, *There's more candy!?* She seems more surprised that there is more candy than who I am going to give it to. "I'm going to go outside and run around a bit." Then I walk out the door.

I go up the stairs to the top area of the deck. I wish I could go to other rooms, but that isn't allowed. I was just really wishing that I would bump into her just like yesterday. I'm roaming around the top area, and I'm looking at everyone with brown hair. I cannot find that girl though. I keep walking around, but still don't spot her, so I find a box near a ledge and sit on it. I don't want to burn myself out by doing nothing, so I just sit down and look at everyone. I can't seem to eye anyone that looks like that girl. The sad thing is... I don't even know her name, so I can't be yelling it across the boat. I want to find her so bad!

<< NOTE FROM EWA>>
Once I feel guilty,
I can't feel better unless
I get rid of that guilt.

I want to say I'm sorry, so I brought a lollipop and everything... Anyway, I keep looking at everyone when I see someone walking towards me. It looks like someone I know. Who is it? HE keeps walking toward me, and I start to notice the face features and notice that it's Filip. *Ugh… Not Filip.* I was sitting there looking for that girl. Not Filip. So, I stand up from the crate I am sitting on and start walking the other way. Then, I casually grab an apple, bite into it and act like nothing ever happened. Filip is nonexistent and I am on my way to meet up with someone really important. *(Truth be told, that girl is pretty important __to me__ so, I guess not all of it is an act).* I hum a cheerful tune, then walk away. Filip looks surprised that I look happy, and I am up to meet somebody. I suspect he wants to give me a lecture about how sorry he is because of the way he acted. *Yeah, oh well, it already happened, there is permanent damage, and there is nothing you can do to fix it.* Sure, an apology might work for some people but NOT FOR ME. FOR ME, you have to be either genuine from the bottom of your heart, or you just don't do whatever someone did to me that hurt me.

I walk down to our room because there is nothing else to do. I want to stay up on the deck and look for that girl, but I don't want to run in with Filip. A Run in with Filip would mean that he knows that I'm avoiding him -> He becomes annoyed and goes into two different scenarios. 1. He goes full on bully mode, or 2. He goes full on fake pathetic mode. Neither is good for me, so I leave.

I wander around, trying to look for that girl again, but can't find her. At this point, I'm tired and want to go back. So, I quit on my journey to find that girl and eat the lollipop myself. I start to go back into the bunk. I'll find her tomorrow.

When I'm in the bunk, I flop down on my bed and open the book that Aleksky lent me. There is literally nothing to do on the boat! As I am reading the book, I wonder what on earth is Rena doing? She didn't follow me today, so I didn't keep an eye on her. I look up to the bunk Rena is supposed to be, but all I see is a note. `I went out with Aleksky.` Nothing else. Just a note that says I went out with Aleksky. Eh, I have some peace and quiet to myself then. I mean that other lady is here with me, but she is silent all the time, so it's fine. Yay. I just keep on reading my book.

Around an hour later, Rena and Aleksky come back.

"Hey, you're back." I say, not really looking up.

"Yeah, we went out to explore the top side." Aleksky says.

"And, it was really fun!" Rena says hyped up.

"Yup, anyway, what did you do?" I say.

"I looked around the top, and got tired, so I read a book." As I am talking to Aleksky, I hear a knock on the door, and a voice says, "Paula! Open the door!" And the woman who was looking like she was knocked out, springs up to the door. She opens it and who do I see? That girl I was trying to find all day today. There's this boy that looks kinda older than me there too.

"Wait! You! You're the girl I bumped into yesterday! What are you doing here?" I half yell from my bunk. I'm totally ignoring that boy.

"I'm here to visit my sister. Paula."

"Wait! You have a sister?" I practically yell at Paula.

"Yes, obviously and a brother." She replies and looks back at the girl.

"Wait! What's your name?" I ask.

"Roksanna" and she looks at Paula and starts to say something, but I cut in.

"I am so sorry about yesterday! Here, have a lollipop."

"Nah, I'm fine, don't worry about it."

"But I'll take it, and the boy takes it away from me. The boy has brown hair like Roksanna, and he's taller than me. (But I feel like he's more childish).

Roksanna looks back at Paula and motions her arm like she is playing something. Paula nods and gets a bag that kind of looks like a misshapen bag. "What's that?" I ask.

"Violin," she says and plops it down on the bunk. Roksanna comes in and sets down a giant suitcase looking thing as well. "What's that?"

"Clarinet. And my sister plays the violin. And Jacub here plays the oboe" She motions to her brother." She sits down on Paula's bunk and clicks open her case. Jacub sits next to her and opens his case as well. They are both adding something to the ends of the pieces. I don't know what that is or what she's doing, but it's pretty cool.

Paula, who is already done getting out her instrument, plays a little piece. I don't know the name of that piece, or how hard it is, but it's pretty. Soon, I hear a different instrument. AND it's Roksanna. While Paula is playing long notes, Roksanna joins. I never heard these instruments, but they are so cool! Then soon after, Jacub joins, showing off his skills. Then, as soon as Jacub runs out of breath, Roksanna takes over, playing an even harder piece. Soon, Roksanna runs out of breath, and Jacub plays a really fast and intricate piece, where I can't even see his fingers moving. Then, Paula motions them to play together, and they nod to each other.

They start playing a simple piece, but it's harmonizing really well. I feel like they've been playing for some time. They are really good! As I'm astounded by the music, Roksanna stops. Rena goes up to her, "That was AMAZING!"

"Aww, Thank you. Can you play anything?"

"No, not really, but Ewa might"

"Who?" Roksanna asks.

"Ewa!" Rena calls me.

"Yeah what?" I answer.

"Can you still play an instrument?" Rena asks.

"I don't know. I never really tried," I answer

"Yeah, you did, 5 years ago when I was two," Rena says making a face that says *I'm sure you can...*

"Well, I did play something, but I didn't really learn, and it was a one-month thing. I'm pretty sure I forgot all about it"

"Wait, you do! What instrument?" Roksanna asks, all hyped up.

"I don't really remember, but you have to blow into it."

"If it's a flute, we have it. Our parents own an instrument shop."

"I don't know the name of it, but I know how it looks."

"Got it" Roksanna says and dashes out of the room.

4 minutes later, Roksanna runs back in and hands me a small looking box. I open it and look at the metal pieces of a flute. I pick it up and assemble it according to memory. Then, I blow into the mouth part. A clear note comes out, and Rena's mouth drops open. I didn't know this was possible. I never could play this note when my school music teacher tried so hard! I wonder how this could happen. Peer pressure?

<<NOTE FROM EWA>>
It was indeed peer pressure.

54

I then proceed to play up and down a scale I don't know the name of. I knew the fingerings by heart, but how was I able to play it? That is a question I would like to ask my music teacher. (She literally quit on me after a month. But we weren't paying her anyway.) Roksanna looks pleased, and Paula looks at me and says the first sentence ever! "You don't seem like a flute person." Ow... I mean I didn't play for a while but, hey, I can play it. I'm surprised. So, as if to prove myself I am good, I start playing random notes and try to make it sound like an actual piece of music. But, as imagined, it sounds like a cat on its deathbed. Well, I mean, I did only learn for a small amount of time, till my teacher quit on me...

"Well, that sounds amazing." Jacob says in a sarcastic tone. Paula on the other hand just looks at me disappointed. Roksanna probably expected it to turn out bad, so she doesn't seem to care. To be honest she even looks a little happy that I can play something. Roksanna gets a piece of paper out of her bag. It has a bunch of weird symbols on it, and she says "Try reading this"

"I can't," I answer, feeling a little embarrassed. I made a big deal about being able to play the flute itself, I didn't think about music. Ugh, now I'm really embarrassed...

```
        <<Note from Music teacher
            that quit on Ewa>>
   She doesn't have any musical talent.
          Heck, she can't even get
       a single note out of her flute!
```

I don't have any "special" musical talent, and I can't even get on top of what people teach me. And here I am mixed into a bunch of people who are musical prodigies. Rena, who I totally forgot about, randomly pipes up with, "What other instruments do you have?"

"Um, I think I may have a recorder?" Roksanna answers not so confidently.

"Oh, yay," Rena says chipperly. I don't want to burden them to let other people use their instruments. Rena doesn't know responsibilities like that and doesn't know what burdens people or not. She just wants stuff. Roksanna shoots a look at Jacub, after which he puts down his oboe and runs out of the room. Soon, he comes back with a recorder that looks a little bent. Rena looks at it and makes a face that says *OMG this is the best thing ever!* Rena says "Thank you! Thank you! Thank you! This is amazing. Can I keep it? Please? Please? Please?"

"Sure, why not." Aleksky says it as she is looking at the recorder.

"Can't use it properly anyways" Jacub says under his breath. Roksanna steps on his foot, and he makes a muffled scream. As this is going on, Aleksky comes into the room with a piece of chocolate in her hands. Her eyes are wide at looking at the 2 new people in the room. She comes into the room and looks at Roksanna and Jacub. "You're that girl that Ewa ran into yesterday, and you... (Looks at Jacub) Who are you?"

"I'm the king of England! No, I'm Jacub. Nice to meet you."

"I'm Aleksky, and I'm guessing that you and this person are siblings?"

"Yup, Paula is the oldest," Paula looks up and waves a little bit.

"I'm second oldest, and Roksanna is the youngest"

"Oh, nice" Then Alkesky goes on top of her bunk. Then, Roksanna proceeds to play something on her clarinet again.

Our Struggle for Normalcy

Jacub joins in on the oboe, and Paula, just noticing the music, joins in as well. They play a really pretty piece, so, as soon as they're done playing, I ask the name. Roksanna replied "I don't even know".

"Ugh" I say, and I climb into my own bunk. I feel like it's getting late, and whatever I do, Roksanna, Jacub, and Paula are going to be practicing their music. So, I'm going to take this as a chance for free bedtime music.

1939-8-9

I wake up and see Roksanna and Paula in Paula's bed. I look around to see Jacub, who is sleeping on the floor with one of the spare pillows. Aleksky and Rena are already awake and getting ready for something. I don't know what they are doing.
"Hey, what are you getting ready for?"
"Oh, um we're apparently stopping at Copenhagen." Aleksky answers.
"Wait, what? Then I have to get ready too!" I yell and start digging through my bag to find clean clothes. As I am rummaging through my luggage, Roksanna wakes up and sees us getting ready. She comes down from the bunk and asks, "What's going on?"
"Apparently we're making a stop at Copenhagen, and I wanted to see what it's like."
"Wait, that's today? Oh, I need to get ready!" Then, she runs out the door. Jacub wakes up because of the commotion.
"What's going on?"
"We're stopping at Copenhagen"

"Oh! I need to go!" Then he also runs out of the room. As soon as he leaves Paula wakes up.

"Can't you be any louder?"

"Nope!"

"And why are you so loud?"

"We're stopping at Copenhagen!"

"Oh, ok. That means I need to get ready." Then she starts to rummage her own bags. I finished getting ready and tied my hair back. "OK! When are we stopping?"

"In about 2 hours." Aleksky answers

"Yeah! And bring your money!" Rena says a bit too hyper.

"Okay, sure?" And I tuck about 100 krone in my bag.

"Oh, and we might be able to get better food there. Apparently, they have more than apples and oatmeal." Aleksky says. I think that she is hyped up for that, but honestly, I am too. Apples and oatmeal get boring. And the apples in here were getting a little mushy.

We go up the stairs and go to the side of the boat to see what is coming next. We lean on the railings and look out and I can see a little speck of land nearby.

"That must be Copenhagen!"I yell.

"Yup! Clear as day!" Roksanna yells from behind me.

"Aah! I didn't know you were here!

"I've been here for a while now. 30 minutes to be exact."

"Oh, cool" I say and look back at the ocean. It's prettier here than out in the place where I could see nothing. Well, I think I can see greens on the land and maybe some more stuff. Then I hear Jacub talking to someone. He's coming this way. I turn around to greet Jacub but see Filip. Huh? Why is Jacub talking to Filip? So, I do the most logical thing possible. I grab

Jacub's shoulder and drag him to the other side of the boat. (Yes, literally drag him) Everyone looks surprised. I don't care. I need answers.

"Who is he?"

"Filip. And OW!"

"I mean how do you know him?"

"He's in the same room. He's also the only one whose age is similar. So, we became friends."

"Really? Him? Of all people?"

"Yes, why?"

"He's a bully and a manipulator. Are you sure you see him as your friend?"

"Ok... I can see that you hate him..."

"Yes, I do. So please can you keep him away from me"

"Sure."

"Thank You." Then Filip walks over to us. He seems worried, and honestly, it seems genuine. It creeps me out. And he was coming closer each second. He was probably coming to check Jacub. But Jacub is right next to me so..., then he came into an arms distance of me, and I really freaked out. So, without making myself seen or heard and not giving anyone time to see my face, I punch Filip with all my might. "OWW," Filip yells. I've wanted to do that for such a long time now.

"What the!" Filip says and glares at me. Oh, well. You don't have your sidekicks to beat me up now. So, I'm safe. The others look shocked except for Roksanna. She seems proud of what I did. I mean, yeah, he deserved it. (For about 2 years, he's been bullying me, so, hah!)

"You deserve it!" And I walk back to Aleksky. She pats me on the back, and I look at the ocean once again. Rena looks at me shocked. I mean she always thought that I liked Filip. But it doesn't matter. Everyone was silent, until Roksanna broke the silence.

"What'd you do that for?" Roksanna looked more shocked than Rena.

"He's a bully and a manipulator. I just punched him for it. That's all" I answer, I want to say more, but that's probably going to take forever.

"Uh... what about forgiveness?"

"Yeah, not happening"

"Um ok."

On the other hand, with Filip and Jacub:

"Dang! Why'd she punch you? It looks like it hurts!" Jacub yells.

"I kinda deserve it..." Filip answers back.

"I did kind of bully her back in our hometown..." Filip adds.

"Oh, like how though... You wouldn't need to be punched like that..."

"Well... lots of different reasons. Ask her yourself if you need details. I don't want to say."

"Ok..."

Back to Ewa and her crew:

"Come on! I want to leave as soon as the boat is on the dock!" Rena yells.

"Fine, fine, but we need to stay in a group, okay? We have to stay together with Aleksky, Paula, Roksanna, me and possibly Jacub," I tell her. I want her to have fun, but if we don't have people telling us when to get back and such, we will probably end up forgetting to go back on the boat. And I don't want that...

"Yeah, I'm tagging along with ya'll and I'll drag Paula and Jacub along," Roksanna says reassuringly.

"Yeah, and don't worry, I'm coming along as well," Aleksky adds. Then we all look out to the sea, looking at the land coming closer and closer. After five minutes of endlessly looking out and trying to see something new, I got bored. So, I turn around to ask Roksanna something. But, before I even realize, Jacub and Filip are here too. "Gah!" I yell in surprise when I first see Filip again, but when I do that, he looks more scared than I am. But I ignore him and go up to Roksanna.

"Hey, we still have time until we arrive, can you play us something?" I ask.

"Uh, sure, let me get my siblings on board," she tells me and walks away.

Soon after, Jacub, Roksanna, and Paula come back with their instruments. Rena looks excited for the music, Aleksky has that proud/anticipating look on her face, and Filip just looks confused. Roksanna and Jacub start to assemble their instruments on the floor, while Paula is adding rosin to her bow. As soon as they are done, they start to play a simple scale.

<<Note from Ewa>>
I learned the basic vocab words for
music.

They are in harmony, and they pull the attention of everyone around them. The people who were just roaming on the top of the boat hear the sound and gather around. They seem surprised by the music, but they don't hate it. They seem to enjoy it even. The song is light and bouncy and easy to enjoy.

As soon as the music ends, everyone claps and claps. I guess there wasn't much music on the boat to start with, but now, there is! Everyone seems happy. Then, I hear the boat clunking on the dock. As if in a queue, the captain yells "Copenhagen!" The siblings look panicked, and they hurriedly put their instruments in their cases, and run down to their bunks to put their instruments away. When they come back, we go off to Copenhagen.

As soon as we get off the boat, we just stare right in front of us. The buildings are all such amazing and bright colors! Our neighborhood didn't have any buildings like this! Wow! I look at the reactions of Rena and the others, and they look as asto I mean, it is a sight you don't see often.

After we just stare at the buildings for a moment, we start walking around. We see shops all around. One of them says INSTRUMENTS FOR SALE. This immediately catches the attention of the siblings, and I can't blame them. They start running to the store and we follow. They all look so happy that they found an instrument shop. As soon as we go in, our faces lit up.

"Oh my god! This is so much larger than what we had!" Roksanna yells.

"This is so cool," Jacub says.

"Nice," Paula says.

Rena looks around at the very first instrument store she's been to. I look around too and see all different kinds of instruments that I have never seen before. There were wooden ones and brass ones. There are stringed instruments and wind instruments. I've never seen so much variety! I only saw the ones that the siblings had! This is so cool!

I look back at the siblings, and they are already testing out the instruments. Roksanna was trying the saxophone, Jacub on the bassoon, and Paula on the cello. They could all make a sound on it. Then, before I even notice, they have made a purchase. Roksanna got the saxophone, and Paula got another violin.

"Why'd you buy that?" Jacub says, stunned. "I understand why Roksanna bought the saxophone, but you already have a violin!"

"It's a Stradivarius violin," Paula says with a grin on her face. "It was a really cheap price, and I think the owner didn't know the full value of this."

"Wait, Stradivarius? Dang!" Jacub says as he motions us to leave the store.

We start walking the streets again with the new saxophone and violin. As we are walking, we start to get hungry and begin looking for a shop or someplace where we can eat something. We eventually find a place with bread in the windows.

"Bread store. Food. Want to go?" I ask.

"Sure" Everyone else replies in unison. So, we go in.

When we go in, the smell of fresh bread hits us. It smells so good! We haven't had this kind of bread since we got on the boat! NICE! We all start roaming around the shop, looking for things to buy. We see a giant baguette on one side of the wall and it's pretty cheap, so we choose to buy it. We pick up three baguettes. One to share now, and two for the boat. We are going to the counter to buy the bread, when I hear someone familiar.

"I'll take the Rugbrod, and a sourdough please," the boy in line in front of us says. He kind of sounds like Frederick, but there's no way it's him. He's still in Poland? Is he not?

"Hello, do I know you?" I ask as I am tapping his shoulder, tapping on his shoulder. I know I shouldn't have, and it was out of line, but still, I need to know.

"Uhh, wait, are you someone from Poland?" He says, not turning around.

"Yes, actually," I answer. He finally looks at me.

"Wait, Frederick?" I half yell.

"Shh!" The woman from the counter hisses at me.

"Okay," I say more quietly. "But, anyways, what are you doing here?"

"I'm going to ride the boat to England. I will be changing boats to get to England. It was faster."

"Frederick! Do you have candy?" Rena yells as she finally comprehends his face and realizes who he is.

"Nah, but I have to start heading to the boat. The only reason I am here is because I need food for the ride," he says as he starts to head out the door.

"Wait! Maybe we'll go with you!" I yell and I follow him. "What boat?"

"Andiamo."

"Wait, we're on the same boat!" Let's go together!" I say and quickly pay for the baguettes.

65

Everyone else looks surprised that I found a friend in the middle of Copenhagen except Rena. Rena is just happy that Frederick is here.

We all start heading back to the boat, but we're not taking the same way we took before. We just walk the other way because well, we have the time, and we want to look around a bit more. We see shops as we walk down, but nothing really piques our interest. I need to use as little money as possible, and I think that Roksanna and Paula wouldn't want to buy anything else. We just keep walking until we have to turn around. Then, after we turn around, there's no store that we really want to go in, so we just walk back to the boat. Because of the new person joining us, we're all in a kind of awkward silence. I really don't like it, so I just come out and say it.

"So, this is Frederick and he's from my school back in Poland!" I say, trying my best to break the silence.

"Oh! That's how you know him!" Roksanna says.

"Yup," I answer back.

"So, anyways, we're going back to the boat, right? We have the food, and I think it's best to save the money instead of just spending it all here," I say.

"Yes, that's a good idea," Paula answers me. Then we keep on walking.

Soon, we see the dock and our boat. We enter the line of people boarding the boat and soon we've boarded as well.

As soon as we are on the boat, we all start heading to our rooms to put our stuff away. Frederick follows Jacub, because they are apparently in the same bunk. Me, Rena, Paula, and Aleksky all go down to our bunk, and Roksanna goes to find her own bunk.

Our Struggle for Normalcy

We put the bread on the floor, and we all just plop down on our bunks. Then we all just start talking nonstop. (Well, me, Aleksky, and Rena to be exact.)

"I can't believe Frederick is here!" I say.

"I know! I wonder if he has more candy!" Rena says hyper. (She got candy from him when I didn't notice.)

"So, he's the guy who's always around your friend group." Aleksky says, finally understanding the whole situation.

"So, he's a friend of yours?" Paula asks. "And he isn't anything like Filip?"

"Yup, almost the exact opposite." I answer back chipperly.

"Who's the dude? I know he's from school, but exactly what relationship do you have with him?" Roksanna says as she comes into the room.

"So, basically, he's a friend from school, and that's about it." I say.

"Really? Nothing else?" Roksanna whines.

"Yes, nothing else" I answer back.

Then I lie down flat on my back, flaring my arms out. I feel a bit tired, and hungry at the same time. So, I walk to the corner of the room and break off a piece of the baguette. I start chewing on that piece, when Rena also gets a piece from the baguette and chews on it.

She then exclaims, "This is so good!"

She genuinely looks like she tasted bread for the first time. And after this reaction, everyone else in the room breaks off a little piece and eats it. And everyone's faces look like it's the best bread ever. Honestly, I've had better, but still!

After everyone tasted the "divine" bread, we forgot what we were talking about, and just plopped on whatever bed was closest and rested? (I don't know. Everyone was just lying down.)

```
        <<A note from Frederick>>
         This is what happened
        when I went into the bunk.
   (Keep reading because there's DRAMA!)
   So, basically, I hate very few people.
 One of them is a childhood bully/friend.
 And coincidently, that person is on this
          boat. Well, good luck.
```

We get on the boat with Ewa and the others, and this guy named Jacub and I have the same bunk, so he's showing me to my room. I want to start a conversation, but I don't know what this person is like, so I start a conversation anyway to find something out.

"So, hello."

"Hello"

"What do you do on this boat?"

"Not much. I sometimes go hang out with my sister's friends and there is one kid who is the same age as me in the room, so, yeah."

"Cool. Is your sister Roksanna?"

"Yup, and Paula."

"Oh, the adultish one"

"Yup."

"Y'all had really weird looking bags that you brung along. What was it?"

"Oh, instruments. We all play it."

"Oh, cool, what instrument?"

"I play oboe, Roksanna plays clarinet, and Paula plays violin."

"Oh, nice. I'm pretty sure Ewa played something a while back."

"Yeah, the flute."

"Wait, how do you know?"

"She plays it now. We're teaching her." That made me burst out laughing.

"Why are you laughing?"

"No, because at one point, she was like," Listen *to my flute playing!"* And it was absolutely horrible!"

"Oh, but she sounds good now! I mean after me and Aleksky trained her…"

"You trained her?"

"She was not that great, so we taught her the basics again and now we are teaching her more!"

"Oh, nice."

"So, do you play anything?"

"Nah, I can sing a bit, but that's the only thing I can do."

"It's fine. Oh, and this is the bunk you'll be staying in."

"Oh, cool!" Jacub opens the door, and I walk in. He motions me to put my stuff on the empty bunk and sit down, so I do as he shows me.

"Anyways, is there anyone else in this bunk?"

"Nope, only me and that other kid named Filip."

"Oh cool." I hated the Filip at my school. I highly doubt it's the same person.

"What is he like?" I need to make sure its not the same person.

"Kinda shy, and really apologetic for what I know." Yup, not the same person.

"Oh, nice." Then I hear the door open, and I instinctively look around and it's the same guy I was fearing. Filip.

"Oh shi—"

1939-8-10

I wake up, and immediately stand up. Everyone else is sleeping to my surprise. I thought everyone would be out of the room by now. I look at the clock in the room and apparently, it's 5:00. I lay back down and read a book till other people wake up.

When I finally hear some rustling, it's 6:30, and it's Aleksky who just woke up. She does her normal routine when she wakes up. She looks around and falls back asleep.

"NO! Don't go back to sleep! It's already 6:30 and I'm bored!" I yell at her, which knocks the sleep out of her system.

"I'm awake!" She says, startled.

"Yeah, and so am I," Paula says, annoyed.

"I'm sorry, but it's already 6:30, and I want to meet up with Jacub and the others!" I say as I start shaking Rena to wake her up. After vigorous shaking for about an hour, she wakes up and immediately starts to get dressed.

"Yes! Someone who is actually getting ready!" I exclaim and get ready myself.

After like an hour of getting people to get ready, we are finally up on the deck. We look out on the ocean looking for something grand and amazing, but there's only the stuff that's always there. Everyone all groans at the same time, they must all be mad at me for waking them up, when there's nothing happening. We walk around the deck a little more, desperately trying to find something cool. Then I see the boys, and I walk up to them, and drag them to where we are.

"How was the bunk?" I ask Frederick.

"Horrid. You know, I have that one person I hate?"

"Yeah,"

"Well, he's in my same bunk."

"Wait…" My brain is firing off with the connections right now.

"That person was Filip?!"

"Yup…"

"Damn! I hate that guy too! I punched him a few days back!"

"Nice!"

"I know! I wanted to do that for years!"

"Wait, years? Did he bully you back in Poland as well?"

"Yeah…"

"Well, Good for you! You punched him! I should have done that a long time ago."

"Well, I did it for you."

"What're you talking about?" Aleksky pops her head in between us.

"Oh, just Filip." I answer back.

72

"Oh, did he bully Frederick as well?" Aleksky asks worriedly.

"Yup" Frederick answers.

"Dang…" Aleksky answers, and she thinks about something for a second and pushes us to join the group.

"Whah! Don't push me so hard!" I yell. Aleksky is pushing me really hard in the direction of the friend group, and incidentally, making me crash into Jacub. We both fall and make a big crash sound. Everyone looks surprised and worried, and Filip looks jealous at the same time.

"Sorry!" I yell. I stand up, help Jacub up and run to Aleksky. As soon as I can reach her, I grab onto Aleksky and shake her.

"Why did you do that!" I yell at her.

"Cuz, you needed a push." She answers back.

"I don't need a push…"

"Yeah, you do"

"Ugh… Just stop. You ship me with literally everyone!"

"Well, yes…"

"Just stop" Then, I walk back to the group, making sure that Aleksky won't push me again. I need to keep sure that she won't make any extra drama for me.

"What are you talking about?" I ask the group.

"Ehh, just more about Filip's bullying history." Roksanna answers casually. I feel like they got used to hearing about Filip's past, and they don't really care as much, because they all kinda saw me punch Filip and all that. They kinda were shocked at the time, but they got over it. Oh, and I just noticed, Filip looks like he is tasting something disgusting right now. He isn't directing the look at me, but at Jacub for some reason. I don't know why this is, but I really don't care about Filip's opinions. Just to make things clear, I shoot him a look that says *I will punch you again.*

We walk around the top of the deck more, because we're bored. Frederick is new here, so he is still getting used to everyone's names, and occasionally gets them wrong. (Especially Roksanna and Aleksky for some reason).

```
<<Note from Frederick>>
They all look the same to me!
What am I supposed to do?
```

While we are walking, we talk about some things, but most of it is just nonsense to pass time. At one point, Frederick brings up the topic of Penguins in tuxedos. This actually starts an argument on if that was a possible scenario.

It went like this:

Frederick: Did you hear about the Tuxedo penguin?

Ewa: Ugh... Not this again...

Frederick: What?

Ewa: I will literally throw you off the boat.

Frederick: I know you won't.

Ewa: Eh, true, but still, don't bring that up again!

Frederick: Eh, I will.

Aleksky: What?

Frederick: The tuxedo penguins!

Roksanna: The what?

Frederick: The tuxedo penguins! They apparently show up to people who have hallucinations. And what they do in their hallucinations are crazy!

Jacub: I'm scared to ask this, but what do they do?

Frederick: Tap dance!

Filip: Huh?

Frederick: This doesn't involve you.

Filip: Ok…

Jacub: So, why do they tap dance?

Frederick: I don't know. They just do.

Paula: And how do you know?

Frederick: Because there's one right there in the corner of the room right now.

Roksanna: Wait? Seriously?

Frederick: No, of course not. How would I be able to see them anyway?

Aleksky: Eh, true.

And that's what happened. Pretty chaotic right? After this, everyone had a pretty good sense of who Frederick was, and we had more useless conversations similar to this. Soon, the conversations ended, and it was starting to get late, so we just went back to our rooms.

1939-8-15

We are finally getting off this boat! I know that the view of the sea is great and all, but if you look at it for a long enough time, it really annoys you. But we are now getting off this boat in 2 hours! We already got to the dock at night, and our group already packed our bags the night before, so we're good to go!

2 hours later...

We all gathered up and went off the boat and onto LAND! We are finally on LAND. (Well, again) We are all supposed to get in a bus that will take us to where our host houses are supposed to be. Then we probably will all split up. So, we're all getting a little emotional with this, but we had fun on the boat, so I'm thankful.

We are waiting on the side of the street looking for a car that will look unusually big to take us. We all have slips with addresses on them that will hopefully tell us where our foster homes are going to be.

After waiting for like an hour, we can finally get on the bus and get going. We all have two copies of the address slips, so we just handed the driver one of the two slips to get to the foster homes. The driver just looks at the slips and immediately starts to drive the bus. We quickly rush to find a place to sit and sit wherever we can. Each seat can seat two people, and so this is the people who sit together. -> Me and Rena, Roksanna and Paula, Jacub and Filip, Frederick and Aleksky.

We all sit in silence. I mean the driver looks a bit mean, and we don't want to get on his bad side. Because if one thing comes to another, we might be kicked out of the bus and told to just walk. I do not want that... I'm already tired, and if I have to walk, I'm going to punch someone.

Rena tries to say something, but I stop her. When she says something, I'm scared that it's going to be something loud or wrong.

"Umphhhh" she tries to say, but my hand is blocking her mouth. "Umshsh Omspsh ahhfps!" She says and she licks my hand.

"Ewww!" I say, kinda loud. As I am saying this, I instinctively move my hand back, which frees Rena. She seems kinda mad at me for blocking her mouth, but I give her a signal that shows that she needs to be quieter. She looks at me with a death glare, but she stays quiet anyways. Aleksky and Frederick are sitting across from us watching the entire thing. And... they burst out laughing.

"What happened?" Jacub asks.

"Ewa, Rena, hilarious," Filip answers, laughing hysterically.

"Oop!" Jacub answers understanding the situation and bursts out laughing too. He probably figured out what happened.

"Shush!" Paula says.

"Ok!" We all say in unison, although half of the people are not involved in this. Then we all kind of sit in silence.

We sit in silence for about 5 minutes until Frederick randomly breaks the silence by saying, "Hey! Look! A tuxedo penguin!"

And I obviously am annoyed by this and kinda yell at him, "There's no such thing as tuxedo penguins!"

Him being used to this, says, "Ummm, yeah there are, can't you see it?"

Roksanna, going along with this, says,"Yeah, I see it! It's really cute!"

Aleksky, knowing how much this bothers me, adds "Awww, I feel bad now because Ewa can't see them! They are so freaking cute!"

Filip wanting to join the conversation, "Awww."

Frederick, still holding a grudge against Filip cuts in, "Again! This does not involve you!"

I am kinda mad but am also amused with this at the same time, so I just close my eyes and go to sleep. But, as I am falling asleep, I can feel the group laughing at the joke.

When I wake up again, everyone else is asleep and I look around to see that the scene outside the window has changed a lot. I try to look behind the bus by looking out the window, and I can't see a hint of the ocean anywhere! I am feeling a little bit of mixed emotions here. I loved the ocean very much, but I did get sick of it.

Soon after looking out of the window, I get tired again and fall back asleep.

"Hey, wake up!" Jacub says, shaking me.

"Huh?" I answer back.

"Wow. She wakes up when you try to wake her. I'm surprised!" Roksanna says.

"Huh? What?" I still don't understand what's going on.

"Girl! You've been asleep the whole time and when we were told to get off the bus, Paula had to carry you! We've been going around trying to wake you up!" Roksanna yells at me. But I still don't get it. To me, it sounded like a bunch of muttering words.

"So, what?" I repeat, sounding clueless.

"WE WOKE YOU UP!" Frederick yells in my ear.

"Ow! I got it now! Geez!" I say, "Dang it! Now I have a ringing in my ear!"

"You kinda asked for it…" Rena says mockingly.

"Don't scream in my ear again please!" I say and get up. Apparently, I was lying down on the ground. I look around me and all of our baggage is out on the road.

"Ugh… What time is it?" I ask

"Around 4 pm," Filip answers.

"Yeah, I wasn't asking you."

"It's 4 pm," Roksanna says.

"Thanks," I answer. I stand up, look around and brush myself off. Half of the people are standing next to me and the other half are sitting on the ground looking bored as ever.

"Ok! I'm awake! Did we get off the bus? And how much do we have to walk to our homes?" I ask.

"Yes, and about 15 minutes," Paula says with a scowl on her face. She must be mad that I was sleeping for so long.

So, we started walking the way that the street sign shows us. We half-expected us to have to split up the second we got off the bus, but apparently, we are heading the same way. *That's surprising*. But no one thinks much about it and keeps walking. I look at my address slip again. 22 West Street CREWE CW25 3QX. Extremely confusing but, that will be our new house. I guess. I keep on thinking.

"Hey! You not listening again?" Roksanna says. This immediately pops me back into reality.

"Huh? Yes... sorry," I answer.

"Come back to Earth!" Rena yells. I mean I have been thinking about random things for some time now...

"Anyways. We're here. Apparently, we're all staying in the same neighborhood. The siblings and Filip are staying in the bluish gray house and you, Rena, and Aleksky are staying in the gray house," Roksana fills me in.

"Oh, Ok!" *That sounds nice!* I think to myself as I start to move the luggage. Rena helps out with moving the small ones. Aleksky grabs her own stuff, and we move it to the front door. The others already moved their stuff while I was moving mine.

Soon, when we moved all of our stuff, we all gave each other one last look and we go up to our new houses.

We step into the house, and we hear a lady running. She comes over to the front door, and she gives us a warm welcome.

"Hi! I'm Mrs. Caddel, and I'll be helping you in England!" She says cheerfully.

"Oh! Hello" I say and quickly introduce myself.

"I'm Ewa, and this is my sister Rena," I say pointing to my sister.

"I'm Aleksky and I am not related to them whatsoever." She says with a grin on her face.

"Oh! I thought you were never going to come! Your rooms are ready. Are you fine with sharing a room?" She asks as she motions us to follow her.

"Yeah! Of course!" I say and follow her up the stairs. The house itself was nice. It seemed like a two-floor building with a small attic and a pretty deep basement. I could see the stairs leading up to the attic and down to the basement. But I follow Mrs. Caddel wherever we are going.

"We're here! There will be pieces of bread for breakfast, and we'll prepare lunch and dinner. We are in the room downstairs and come down if you need anything!" she says and opens the door for us. We go in and it seems like a pretty good room. There are 4 beds by the wall and a desk and a bookshelf. There was one lamp by the side of the room, but that was about it. But honestly it was better than we thought, and it was cozy too. So, we all put our things aside and plopped onto the beds and just stared up at the ceiling.

"Hey, so we made it huh?" I say.

"Yup," Aleksky and Rena say just to go into silence.

I'm going to sleep," I say.

"Same here," Aleksky says. Rena makes a snoring sound and we all just fall asleep.

<<Note From Roksanna>>
SO, we're finally in England,
we're in our houses. Basically, what
happened was this.(I'll talk in bullet
points to make it short)->

81

- Went into the house.
- Met a really crazy person named Mrs. Barlowe.
- Mrs. Barlowe took us to the dinner table.
- Gave us a giant breadstick.
- Ate the giant breadstick.
- Took us to our rooms
- Unpacked. Went to sleep.

<<Note from Frederick>>
So basically, I'm stuck with Filip.
This is what happened.
Me: Yay! I'm here!
But what are you doing here?
Filip: I'm staying here as well.
Me: Oh, Shi- (And I don't remember anything else. When I finally got conscious of my surroundings again, I was in my bed.)

1939-8-16

I wake up, and no one else is awake. The clock says it's around 8:00 and I don't really care. I'm hungry and I start heading down to get bread. The lady who's house we're in said that I can get bread in the morning. Well, more so in a way that was like *BREAD IS YOUR BREAKFAST!* So, like ok.

When I go downstairs, I see a bag of toast and bread rolls, so I grab one and look for some jam. I can't see anything nearby, so I just bite into the bread. It's really good. It has a buttery taste, and a really interesting flavor. I never had this kind of bread before!

I take another with me and start heading upstairs. I know where the others are staying, so I can probably meet up with them. When I finally get upstairs, I take some fresh clothes out and change with Rena and Aleksky. They just casually put on new clothes and follow me. I guess they got used to it on the boat.

They are still kinda tired, but they follow me anyway. As soon as we are outside the door, I have to rely on my memory on where they are going to be. "Ummmmm I'm just going to knock on whatever door is near," I say as I walk to a bluish gray house and knock.

"Hello, is Roksanna or Frederick here?" I need to ask for either of them because they are in different houses and the others are either staying with Roksanna or Frederick.

"Yes, Roksanna is here, I'll call her down. And while you're at it, do you want some bread?" The lady says.

"Actually, yes please," I answer. I want to give something to the others to eat. They must be starving. I get the breadstick and hand it to Rena and Aleksky. They take it from my hand and don't eat it. I guess they weren't hungry after all. I then proceed to wait for the woman to come back.

Soon, when she did come back, she was with a pajama wearing Roksanna who was being dragged by Paula. Paula looked annoyed and Roksanna looked like she was still asleep.

"Take her. While you're at it, take Jacub too. I'm going to enjoy the peace and quiet," Paula says and gives us Roksanna. She then goes upstairs to grab Jacub. The woman comes back with more bread and gives each of us a piece. She then seems to remember something and goes back into the house. Soon Jacub comes out, fully dressed and not sleepy at all. He then takes Roksanna from us, straightens her up and hits her on the head.

"Ahh! What!" Roksanna says, waking up.

"Wake up and get dressed," Jacub says.

"All right, give me a minute," Roksanna says and goes upstairs.

Soon, she comes back fully dressed. She comes out the door to see us all waiting for her.

"Come on. Let's go get the others," I say and head to another random house to knock on the door. *Please, luck be on my side!* The house I knock at has a greenish grayish color. When I knock, no one comes out. I knock again, and this time a really nice-looking person comes out. They seem to look like they are in their 40s or so.

"Hello?" he says.

"Hi, does anyone with the name of Frederick stay here?" I ask.

"No, sorry. I'm not taking care of anyone." Then as he says this, he slams the door. Well, he at least looked kind. We are all kind of shocked because of this but, we don't mind. We all know there are unkind people in this world. I mean that's how wars like this one happen right?

Anyways, we head to the next house. It has a full gray color, and I'm begging for luck again. *Please luck! Help me out now!* I knock on the door and Filip opens the door. As soon as I see him, he says, "Hey? What are you doing here?" I proceed to ignore him and just call out really loud. "FREDERICK! KILLER UNICORNS AND PENGUINS!" Then I hear running footsteps coming down. Then I hear this, "Where! Where! Where! Where!" He says, running down the stairs.

"Nowhere. Come on, let's go." I say and basically drag him out of there. So, we have all of the crew now. Well, Filip is tagging along even though I hate it. I plan to go to a nearby park that I saw on the way here. It looked nice and we might be able to get more info about the place we are staying in. Yes, we could ask our foster parents, but I prefer to do my research with my friends. I mean it was great to work with Grethe, Greta, Hailee, and Anders. I do miss them, but I have new friends now! It should be great! Right?

We all start heading to the park. Many of us have a breadstick in our hand that was given to us by Mrs. Barlowe. We chew on that while we go to the park. A lot of things happened but they were all nonsense.

This is basically what happened:

Frederick: Anything happen?

Me: Nah

Aleksky: Nope

Roksanna: Mrs. Barlowe is crazy about food, but she's nice.

Rena: Yeah, not much.

SILENCE

Arrive at the park.

Frederick talks about monsters under the mountain:

[illegible handwritten/squiggle text — five lines]

Others: oh wow

Me: Good grief

I don't remember the rest. We went home after that.

1939-11-10

Everything is normal, I guess. We have enough food every day and once in a while we get to see the siblings perform some kind of song. I also have gotten way better at flute than I thought. I can now play some songs that Roksanna randomly gives me. But I'm nowhere near at their level though. The newspaper said that Hitler invaded Poland, and we didn't get contact from our parents for some time. When we finally did get the letter, they were evacuating to another place that they didn't inform us about in the letter. Most of the contents in the letter were the same. They're fine as of late, it's safer for them to evacuate. They won't specify where in case this letter gets taken away.

I think the war is getting worse and worse. The reality is setting in little by little now. There are bomb alarms that go off once in a while, so we have to go into the bomb shelter that is in the basement of Frederick's house.

Honestly, too little has happened in the past three months. I mean, I was just doing whatever I could with the time I had. We didn't even go to school! (That is the one part I am happy about though)

But, back to the present. I'm going to get groceries for Mrs. Caddel. We need potatoes, flour, tomatoes, and we can get candy if we want. I mean, the normal stuff we need to do. I get bored when I'm out shopping alone, so I dragged Rena and Aleksky along and they don't seem to mind. They're just happy about the possibility of getting candy. When we get to the shop, we shop really fast. We get all the things we need and choose a candy for ourselves and come out of there. We didn't need to be there for a long time. We just get the needed stuff and come out.

We walk back to the house, give Mrs. Caddel the groceries, and we head out again. We can have the remaining day to ourselves until we have to go to the city to get something. But, in that case, Roksanna and the others are going to come with us. They like going into the city, and luckily Today is one of those days where Mrs. Barlowe, Mrs. Caddel and Mr. Fletcher's plans synchronize. So, the gang gets to go out altogether!

I'm waiting for the bus to come. Everyone else is waiting with me. The bus is going to take us to the middle of the city, and we'll get off, and we're free to look around as we want.

Finally, the bus comes, and we all get in. It seems like ages since I saw this bus. I mean this is the same bus we took when we were coming here from the dock.

We go on the bus, and when the bus starts to move, nothing really happens. We're not silent, or anything, just we don't talk about anything important. Just stuff about what we want to do when we get to the city.

The bus stops and we all get off.

"Be careful and be back here by 9:00 to catch the bus again," Mrs. Caddel says and leaves. Mrs. Barlowe follows her, and Mr. Fletcher just gives Filip and Frederick a look that says *Follow your friends and you'll be fine.*

So, off we go. We really have no exact destination, but we are just going to start heading to random places for food. We need to get some stuff to eat. I see a shop close by. It apparently sells sausages, and well, why not. So, I ask the others if they want to eat there, and they agree. So, we enter the shop. It seems like a harmless shop, and well, the sausages are cheap, and the owner looks nice. While Aleksky, Frederick, Filip, Jacub, Paula, and I buy food, Roksanna goes out to get something and Rena follows her because she needs to use the restroom. Roksanna just wants to visit a nearby bookstore. She is going to take Rena to the bathroom then bring her back, so we trusted her.

By the time the man gives us our sausages and soup, we hear a bombing alarm. This was becoming more of a common thing these days, so we just did what we always did. The shop owner showed us to the basement under the shop and told us that we should stay in there to be safe until the bombing alarm was over.

"You bought our product, which means that you are our customer. We have the responsibility to keep you safe as long as you are in the shop," he says as we are halfway down the stairs to the basement.

Once we are in the basement, we start to eat the food we just bought. We are hungry after all, so we eat the food in the basement while waiting for the bombing to end.

Two, maybe more hours pass, and the danger is eventually over. We come out of the basement carefully, wondering if the shop is still intact. Luckily the bombing alert came from the other side of town, and it was just a precaution.

When we come out of the shelter, we start to head to the bus stop where we are supposed to meet with the adults. We don't talk all that much on the way there. When we get to the bus stop and I instinctively wait for Rena to take my hand, she's not there. I look around to see if she is with any of the others, but I don't see her.

"Rena's not here," I panic.

"Wait, she isn't?" Aleksky says.

"Maybe she's still in the shelter," Filip says.

"No, she went outside to use the bathroom," I say, the panic in my voice rising by the second.

"Oh, she must have gone into a different shop while we were in the shelter at the shop," Paula says.

"Oh, yeah. Can we go search for her?" I ask.

"Yeah," Frederick says and all of us start to head back to the shop we came from.

When we get to the shop, we start to look around and go to different shops asking if anyone has seen a kid who is short and talks a lot. All of them say no, until we come to a little cafe.

The owners say, "Oh, she left with this man who was also in the shelter. He said that they were apparently neighbors, and they knew each other." After they say this, we immediately think of that rude man who closed the door on us three months ago.

"Oh, God. I'm going to tell Mrs. Caddel about this. Maybe she can help," I say and start to head to the grocery store that she went to.

"Oh, yeah. Maybe that person is there too," Aleksky says, and starts to walk with me. I'm still panicking, and I'm trying so hard to not go into my talking-to myself-mode. We keep on walking to the grocery store.

Our Struggle for Normalcy

<< Note from Rena >>

So, I got lost. Well, so I went to a random shop near me. I kinda lost Roksanna in the crowd that was running into shops after the bomb alarm. I just thought to myself, I'll find her when the alarm is done. I just need to stay quiet for a while. And I know where to go when the alarm is over. THE BUS STOP!

But I couldn't get to the bus stop because I met that person who shut the door on us like a few months ago.

So, I was in the shelter, trying my best to stay quiet, but I just had to talk nonsense with the person next to me. I started talking about Tuxedo penguins just like Frederick would. And surprisingly the person listened to the whole thing with interest. When I was finally done talking, I looked at his face and it was the man who slammed the door. Well, he seemed nicer now. His name was Mr. Aze. Anyways, he noticed that my friends were not here, so he asked me if I wanted to be taken to the neighborhood, and he could drop me off.

And that was great for me. I could easily go home without any trouble. So, when the alarm was over, I followed him out and was heading home.

```
<< Note from Roksanna >>
      DON'T FORGET ME!
   So, what I did was ->
```

- Took Rena to the bathroom
- She said that she could handle going back alone.
- I went to the book shop
- Bomb Alarm
- Went into the shelter.
- Met a family friend and am staying with them now.

TWO HOURS LATER

We keep looking around town while we are heading to the grocery store to find Mrs. Caddel. When we finally reach the grocery store, we catch sight of our foster parents. I run up to them in a hurry to tell them what has happened. But when I get closer, I can see a kid who is about the same age as Rena. *Wait, is that her?* I think to myself as I basically run to the girl. And YES! It is her. She is with Mrs. Caddel and this man next to her. They are talking about something. When Rena sees me, she looks relieved.

"Sorry, I met Mr. Aze and he took me to Mrs. Caddel. He is actually nice!" Rena says and she begins to babble on about what happened.

When she is done. I am so glad I found her that I forget about everything else. I even forget that everyone else is here. Mrs. Caddel tells us that we are going back now, because she bought everything that they needed, and the bombing alarm was a little chaotic for all of us.

Our Struggle for Normalcy

We start to head to the bus stop, and soon, the bus arrives. We all get on, taking our seats just the same. We start to talk randomly about what happened. And soon we are back at our houses. We begin to head into our houses, when Jacub yells, "Hey? Is Roksanna staying with you guys today?"

"No, I thought she was with you!" I yell back.

"Well, she's not!" Jacub says.

"She wasn't in the bus either," I say, as I start to head over to their house.

"Well, then, where is she?" Paula asks.

"I'm going to check with Filip," Jacub says as he starts to go towards Filip and Frederick's house.

Soon, Frederick and Filip are out in the street as well.

"No, she's not here," I hear Filip say.

"Well, she went to the bookstore, before the alarm. I didn't see her after that. And I mean we were kind of busy trying to look for Rena and everything, so we did kind of forget her," Frederick says.

"Well, it's late and even if Roksanna was near here, we would have to wake her. Let's go back to town tomorrow. She's not as young as Rena, so she probably didn't go after random people," Aleksky says.

"Yeah, probably a good idea because we are all tired, and used up most of our energy today looking for Rena. I'm going to tell Mrs. Barlowe. She will probably help us find Roksanna." And Jacub leaves, going inside his house.

1939-11-11

I wake up early the next day with a feeling more of dread than apprehension. I was thinking all last night of the ifs of not finding Roksanna.

Rena will probably stay inside because she said and I quote, "I know where Roksanna is. But as far as that information goes, she's still in the bookshop saying, 'this place has sheet music!' and I also don't think that she was thinking much about the rest of us because before I left for the bathroom, she was talking with these people with giant backpacks like those ones with instruments who looked like they just came from the palace." I mean, that's the amount of information that we have to work with. Not much, but we can still work with it. I wrote all the important details in the bullet list on a small sheet of paper.

DETAILS TO FIND ROKSANNA

- Went into the bookstore.

- Talked with these people who looked like buskers.

- PEOPLE - one of them had an extra-large case, brown hair looked around 6 feet (Male). Smaller case, blond hair, looked around 5 foot (Female) Another brown hair and looked like the twin of the six-feet guy, but shorter. (Male)

- Roksanna apparently said something like "So nice to see you again."???

I want to be able to get to Roksanna, but I'm not exactly sure how to find her. At least I have the information. I go outside with Aleksky and see that everyone is waiting outside. Everyone except Mrs. Caddel and Rena.

We head onto a bus into the city, hoping to find Roksanna there. As expected, there isn't much chatter. When we get to the city, we head to the bookstore first. We are hoping to find Roksanna there, but no dice. We search and search and even ask all the workers in the bookshop, but there's no one who knows the exact whereabouts of Roksanna. The closest thing we got was the information we already know. The, "She went with these buskers."

We have to search harder. We go into all the nearby shops. And we find nothing.

Until, we go into this inn, where the owner says "Oh, they stayed here last night. They were headed out of town." So now we know where to go next. Out of town. But we don't know which way they went. I mean, we know that they were in this inn last night, so that's a good thing, I guess. All the while we are getting more information on the whereabouts of Roksanna, we can see the anxiousness creeping up on Jacub and Paula. For the first time, we are seeing the side of Paula which isn't *I'm annoyed and please leave me alone.*

We go into more shops and get nothing. So, we get onto another bus that heads out of town. We don't know where they are right now, so we are going to head north. If they have no idea who Roksanna is or where she is, then we will head to different towns.

The bus is coming in about an hour. Sadly, we missed the bus that left right before we came to the bus stop. But this means we have enough time to comprehend everything and think things through. Without anyone talking, the bus came. We silently board the bus and keep silent the whole ride. It is strange because I expect Frederick to say something to lighten the mood. But he doesn't say anything. He actually seems to have some common sense and the ability to read a room for once. I'm surprised. I didn't expect things to turn out like this. I was really hoping that fate would connect us to where Roksanna is in the town we already were in. But, again, no dice.

We were at the town nearby in what seemed like days. I never knew that silence could make time feel longer by a lot. I mean I guess I never was in full silence. My head was always rambling about something every day. We all get off the bus and start going into all the shops that looked like they might be open. It is getting late, so a lot of the shops are starting to close. But if needed, we will search all night for Roksanna. I mean, she will have to have someplace to stay the night, and I think that these inns will be open all day and night in case people want to leave in the middle of the night.

We ask all the workers of the stores that are open. Mrs. Barlowe and Paula got into a bar to ask a few things because we are not allowed to go in. When she comes back, she looks like she has some information for us. She says, "So, basically, they did a gig here with their busking. Apparently, they hauled in a crowd. So, the owner was so thankful that she got them a gift. And they mentioned where they were going next. The owner said, 'They said that they were heading more north from here.'"

Oh! Thank God! I think to myself as I leave the place. Jacub seems to be lost in thought when he whispers something into Paula's ear. She seems like a lightbulb just turned on and was lost in thought as well. Aleksky is very intent on knowing what was going inside their heads, so she asks "So, anything good?"

"Oh, just that they remind me of some family friends," answers Jacub.

"Oh, ok." Then we just keep walking.

It is getting late, and we know where to search tomorrow, so we head home.

1939-11-12

We are all ready to go. In a second, we are on the bus, and in the next, at the town we wanted to go to. We're hoping to find Roksanna here. We go into inns because she had to stay in one, right? We ask everyone possible until we get an answer. We are heading closer to the heart of the town, when we hear a clarinet playing. I for a minute think this is Roksanna, but there are a lot of clarinet buskers in the world, right? But it wouldn't hurt to check.

I start to run toward the sound of the music, but Jacub is one second earlier than me. He is running at the sound of the music as soon as it is audible. I catch sight of Roksanna doing some crazy solo at the front of an instrument shop. I start to sprint. When I see her, I feel a huge wave of relief hitting me.

I approach really close to her and she still doesn't notice us. I hug her as soon as she is in reach, and then she finally notices us. Her clarinet squeaks and Jacub is hugging her as well. The others come running. They see us and all start to tear up. We are all in a big hug when we see them: The people that Roksanna supposedly was following.

"So… Big emotional crowd today, Rocks?" The taller man says.

"Yup," Surprisingly, Roksanna is the only one not crying. I guess she wasn't that scared after all.

"What were you thinking!" Paula says, snapping out of all the emotion.

"Oh, well, I got lost after the alarm, and didn't know where to go, so I walked around, and I met them! Remember Antoni, Zofia and Igor?" She points at each of them. The tallest man is Igor, the shorter man is Antoni and the woman is Zofia. "They were in the same busking crew as mom!" Roksanna says as we all start to stop crying. We didn't even have time to tell her that we were all really worried.

"So, they are them!" Jacub is trying to sound normal, but we can all hear his voice crack.

"Yup, and they heard my skill now, which is way better than when I was 7, so they were like 'Join the busking for a while' and I was like 'yeah,'" Roksanna says, and as she starts to babble on a little more, Paula blocks her mouth. "No"

"Why not." Roksanna says as she pulls Paula's hand free.

"Too young. Maybe in like 5 years," Paula says.

"She's good enough and mature enough to join us," Antoni says.

"Yes, she is good enough, but not mature enough," Paula says. And she adds, "You will go back home with us because you gave us all a panic attack when we saw you weren't there with us."

"But I kinda want to stay. We were really popular at that bar too," Roksanna says and at the end of the sentence, her voice starts to get whiney.

"No," Paula says and takes the clarinet out of her hands, disassembling it.

"Well, technically Paula is the legal guardian here, so we can't argue," Zofia says.

"Ok, let's go," Paula says, practically dragging Roksanna along.

Jacub shows a sorry look to the buskers and walks toward Paula. The buskers are like, what the hell happened and that went by so fast! Then they snap back to reality, and Zofia says this, "We'll go where you go. We don't really need to be here anyway."

I don't even fully understand what went on at the last minute, but I guess we're going home now. And the buskers are coming with us.

A few hours later, we are on the bus back home. We hear Roksanna get yelled at by Paula. We kinda yell at her too for the amount of anxiety she gave us. One hour later, we are home. We all go our separate ways, and the buskers join the siblings at their house.

1939-11-13

<<Note from Roksanna>>

- I got yelled at by Paula again for running away.
- Then, our family friends came to my rescue.
- They said that it was mostly their fault.
- They tried to convince Paula to let me join them
- Paula said all polite, "Maybe when she's older"
- They kinda looked like they lost their purpose and said "Oh, ok, we just want to tell you all the things we can do for her and such and help you understand.
- Then they went on about what they did, and the most significant parts were that they made money by playing for bars, inns and more.

They never stayed in one place for more than a month. That kinda lost it for me. Although I love traveling, I like having a home and staying now and then.

- Then I said no thanks. Which surprised Paula and Jacub quite a bit.
- Then they left. They just said, "Thanks for letting us stay for so long and left."

When I wake up, I hear the siblings playing their music outside. I mean, that is pretty normal, but I didn't expect them to be playing this early in the morning. Wait, no it's 9:00. So, not that early.

I go out and see them playing their usual piece, and I go near them. Then as I go closer, Roksanna starts to play her solo, followed by Jacub. Jacub is playing low notes and supports Roksanna as she goes into full jazz. I thought their piece was classical music. Huh? It sounds nice.

When they're done, I clap. Roksanna looks at me weird, and I notice that I'm still in my pajamas. I run back to the house, change and come back out. They are playing a second piece now and Filip and Frederick come out. To my surprise, Filip is singing something in French that I don't understand. It fits the classical piece.

Soon, Rena and Aleksky come out as well, drawn out by the music. We then just jam to the music.

We just listen and chill for a few minutes, and I remember my flute and run to get it. I haven't practiced for a really long time, so I hope I didn't forget. I start out with a simple scale and try to join them. I can't, well, they are on a different level, so I just jam again. We all listen to the music as more people come out. Mrs. Caddel, Mr. Caddel, Mrs. Barlowe, Mr. Aze, and Mr. Fletcher all stand and watch us jamming and playing music.

Everyone who plays, as soon as they are done, stands up (if they weren't already standing yet) and bows. We clap and then start chattering.

"That was amazing!" Mr. Fletcher says.

"I never knew that they played this great!" Mrs. Barlowe says with a face of pride.

"You sing?" I ask Filip while ignoring the adults.

"A little bit. Just as a hobby," He says, trying to act like he never sang before in his life.

"Ok! You are joining them from now on!" I say and push Filip to the siblings. Then we start to chatter about nonimportant things again.

After some chattering, it's already time to go inside. We forget about lunch and just keep talking. Then after that, it is pretty boring. We go inside, eat dinner, and come back out for one last song, then go to bed. I hope days like this can last.

EPILOGUE: *eight years later*

"Come on Rena. I know you hate me because I'm the boring sister, but I do have legal guardianship, so you can't complain," I say as I basically pull Rena away.

"I can go home by myself you know. And I have friends," Rena says, trying to push away from me. She is 16 now. I am 21. I am technically an adult, the war is over, and Rena is enjoying her high school life to the fullest. Her high school life isn't that much different from my middle school life, just that she lost the chatter part of her character.

"Come on. Mum's waiting." Mama and Father came back, and I started to call Mama, mum because well, that's what everyone is calling their Mama in England. I gave into peer pressure. Father is working here in a nearby hospital and Mama teaches Polish in a nearby academy. We all still live in Mrs. Caddel's house.

"Ugh." Rena says as she is slowly walking with me. Showing with all her motions that she doesn't want to go home with me.

"Fine, go with your friends." I say and walk out fast.

A few of Rena's friends walk out of the school finding Rena.

"Rena! Hey! Wait up!" Says one of Rena's friends that I don't bother to know who.

I walk home quickly. I try not to be noticed by Rena's classmates and friends.

A few minutes later, I'm home getting ready for dinner. Mum is already halfway done with dinner and Rena is probably gonna be an hour late. I casually slide in next to Mum and start to help with anything that is involved in cooking. Then I yell out, "Frederick! Come set the table!"

"Yeah, give me a second!" And then I hear running footsteps down the hall. He comes and sets the table, in record speed, and goes back to his room.

I help Mum with the cooking for a bit, and I head to my room as well. It's going to be some time before Rena comes in, but dinner will start in like 10 minutes.

Before I even notice, I'm in my room and 8 minutes pass. I don't even remember what I was doing. But I do know that a long time has passed, and I should go to dinner.

When I get to the dinner table, everything is set, and all it needs is people. I yell out to Father and Frederick, and they come in soon after. We all sit and eat, talking about our day, and wondering about what will happen tomorrow. Then Rena comes in through the front door. She looks happy, and she also sits down at the dinner table, and eats, but quietly. We all finish our food soon after and go to our rooms.

I get to my room and quietly stare up at the ceiling. I'm still sharing a room with Rena and Aleksky went back to Poland with Filip. And the buskers came back to England to do a gig a few years ago, and that time Roksanna, Jacub, and Paula joined them because they were older than 18 at the time. And Frederick is staying in the other room at the end of the hallway.

I think that things turned out pretty well, but I can't be sure. I'm glad everything turned out the way it did.

About the Author

Born in Seoul, South Korea and now living in Boston, Yujeong Lee is a teenager who loves exploring stories—whether through the philosophical humor of Peanuts or the wide worlds of fiction. Moving across cultures has made her very observant of how teenagers are when they are far from home. This inspired the theme in her novel, *The Struggle for Normalcy* in 1939. Outside of writing, she enjoys spending time with her friends and animals, and aspires to become a veterinarian while continuing to write stories that reflect the voices of young people.